The
Three Red Flares

The
Three
Red Flares

DAVID DIVINE, *pseud.*

arthur D. Divine

Thomas Y. Crowell Company
NEW YORK

Frontis and map on page 28 by Rus Anderson

First published in the United States of America in 1972.
Copyright © 1970 by DAVID DIVINE

Designed by Jill Schwartz

MANUFACTURED IN THE UNITED STATES OF AMERICA

L.C. Card 72-78280
ISBN 0-690-82357-6

1 2 3 4 5 6 7 8 9 10

To Caroline Jane Keir

Chapter ONE

"WHERE'S your bike?" Peter's voice conveyed with brilliant simplicity a sense of deep personal injury, a note of unbearable urgency and a statement of the unarguable fact that girls will almost always let you down in crisis anyway.

"At home," said Mig placidly.

"Why?"

"Because I came by bus." Mig spaced the words out slowly and distinctly as if she were talking to a small child.

"I know *that*. I saw you get off. Why this morning of all the mornings there are?"

"Because"—Mig's voice became irritatingly helpful and sympathetic—"because Mother's picking us up. Remember? Picking us up because Clint's coming. Remember? And Clint will have his scuba suit and his flippers and his spear gun and a mass of books and one suitcase at least and . . ."

"Shut up!" In desperation Peter permitted himself to descend to sordid colloquialism and waved an exasperated arm.

"Distraught," said his sister, "just plain distraught. What d'you need it for?"

"I must have it. I must have a bike! I can't get there without it by ten-thirty and I must get there by ten-thirty—I must!"

"Where?" demanded Mig, not unreasonably.

"Mr. Ramidge's."

"Isn't he here?" Mig looked with a faint expression of sur-

prise over to the great bulk of the cathedral that rose behind
them like a cliff, propped up with scaffolding and enormous
girders and vast baulks of timber.

"*Old* Mr. Ramidge," said Peter with a frantic air. "I've got"
—he looked hurriedly at his wristwatch—"fourteen minutes
to get there, wasting all this time looking for you and talking
. . . and you know what they say about him!"

"I didn't know you'd asked again . . ." began Mig.

"I hadn't." Her brother interrupted her with asperity. "I
didn't know anything about it. Mr. Ramidge left a message to
come to the Master-Builder's office as soon as I got here. But
I went to the Paradise dig first and I didn't get his message
until after ten, and then he said that his father hadn't men-
tioned us for a week, but this morning at breakfast he'd suddenly come up with this, and that I was to be there at half-past
ten and not a minute later. It had to happen like this! It just
had to!"

"Taxi?" said Mig.

"I've only got three bob. You?"

"One and six. No taxi." Mig stepped back and looked along
the side of the Bell Tower. "Miss Pringle's bike? No, won't
do; she always goes home for a snack at eleven. She'd be mad.
She's set in her ways. Who else has a bike? Mr. Strickland . . ."

"He's working over in the Royal Chantry. It would take
minutes to find him and then to find the bike wherever he
keeps it."

"I know where he keeps it," said Mig calmly. "Between the
Works office and the wall. You take it! I'll go and ask his permission afterwards."

"And if he says no?"

Mig's voice suddenly became grown-up. "I shall use my
charm. Beat it!"

Peter stood irresolute for a moment. "I'm scared, Mig."

"Of Mr. Strickland? I can manage Mr. Strickland."

"Of Old Mr. Ramidge."

"He's ninety-two," said Mig firmly. "He can't eat you."

"Can't he? He scared the pants off the Dean. Anybody who can scare the Dean can scare me."

"Listen!" Mig became intensely practical. "If we're right, he's got half the information. If his son's right, he's spent a lot of his life trying to find the other half. We know that *we* have the other half. Trade. It's simple—and remember to call him 'sir.' After all, he *is* ninety-two. Stop talking and get Mr. Strickland's bike!"

She watched him wheel the bicycle across a lull in the westbound traffic stream, mount and begin to pedal furiously toward Chichester Cross. West Street was brilliant in the morning sun and the south face of the Bell Tower was like bright silver against the blue of the hot-weather sky. In this brightness it was impossible to see the flaking and the decay of the ancient stone. Mig had a special love for the Bell Tower.

When Peter disappeared, she turned and walked down past the west front of the cathedral toward the cloisters to search for Mr. Strickland. She had decided that she'd better look demure. Mr. Strickland, she was sure, did not really appreciate the young and he might be awkward if by any mischance he needed his bicycle before lunch. She couldn't even guess how long Peter would be. Nobody could ever guess anything about Old Mr. Ramidge.

It wasn't true, of course, as the Dean sometimes claimed when he was being frivolous, that he'd tried to prop up the spire single-handed when it fell in 1861, but he *was* so old that he was a part of the cathedral legend, unpredictable, irascible, at times—from his son's accounts—absolutely and furiously unreasonable. Everybody in the cathedral remembered him with awe, even those who had never had anything

to do with him. He'd been a part of its crumbling, threatened
existence for much more than half a century and for another
twenty years his advice had had to be asked on every major
point after his son had succeeded him as Master-Builder.
Young Mr. Ramidge—he was in his early sixties—was at least
as scared of his father as was the Dean.

She decided that she would like to grow old like that herself,
to live until she had years enough to be angry with everybody
—and get away with it. It would be infinitely more fun than
growing old graciously and being put upon by grandchildren.
Florence Nightingale, for instance, or Queen Elizabeth. What
was it "good" Queen Bess said when she was dying on her
heap of cushions and Cecil tried to insist on her going to bed?
Serenely she recalled the words: "Little man, is 'must' a word
to use to princes?"

Turning at the corner of the Bishop's chapel, she went in
at the doorway into the West Alley. Mr. Hotchkiss, the Pre-
centor, was just coming out with a lady whom Mig did not
recognize. She greeted him with her best version of a shy
smile. As they, in turn, went through the doorway she heard
him say—his voice carried beautifully: "Such a nice quiet
child."

Chapter TWO

THE footsteps under the dark roof of the cloister stopped and a voice said, with an air of accustomed wariness: "You told me I'd find you in Paradise. Where do I find you? In a hole—digging."

Without turning, Mig answered, positively: "This is Paradise. You're late, Clint."

"British Railways." The American boy got his shot in before the girl could establish too much ascendancy. "Even you can't stand up for the Southern. Why's it called Paradise?"

"Always has been," said Mig with an insufferable air of logic. "Buy yourself a handbook to the cathedral. It's properly marked." She grunted in a strictly unladylike manner and freed a fragment of red pottery that had been claiming her attention. Straightening herself, she half turned and grinned at the boy. "Second thoughts, I'll lend you ours. I'm feeling generous. I'm glad you've come, Clint."

Clinton looked at her suspiciously. He knew his Mig reasonably well now. "What sort of trouble are you in this time?"

"No trouble," answered Mig airily, "but you were the only character we knew who could use a scuba suit properly—we're only just beginners, and"—she threw in the words a shade too casually—"keep his mouth shut."

"Just where does one use a scuba suit in a cathedral?" demanded Clinton ironically.

"It ties up. Oh yes, in a manner of speaking it ties up." Mig was being deliberately obscure. It was clear that she wasn't giving anything away, and Clinton knew her much too well to press, even when, quite unfairly, she added: "Stop arguing and get down to some work!"

Instead he put his leg over the broken parapet of the tracery. "Not there," said Mig hurriedly. "Go back to the Paradise Wicket and come in the proper way, and don't walk across the graves. They"—she hesitated a little at the irreverence—"they get gooseflesh."

The American boy walked back admiring the shiplike ribs of the long chestnut roof. The tracery of the high arcade was old and worn and full of time. As he slipped through the wicket gate he became aware again of the great spire, soaring so splendidly now against the sky that its finial and the great cock perched upon it seemed a danger to the orderly cumulus cloudlets that had drifted across the blue. Below the spire the tower, straight, clean-lined and majestic, was like a castle keep. He kept glancing up at it almost under compulsion as he picked his way along what he hoped were the proper paths between the tombstones. There was little enough to go by.

Arrived at Mig, he asked quietly: "What *are* you digging for? And why here?"

"This and that," said Mig evasively. "This is a mixed-up site. Regnanses deep down, Romans in the middle, medieval above, and bits of Victorian beer mugs on top—all mixed up at least three times like a Christmas pudding, once by the Romans, once by the Normans when they built the cathedral, and once by Sir Giles Gilbert Scott when he rebuilt the tower."

"Why?"

"It fell down," answered Mig simply. "I'll show you the pictures when we get inside."

He stood quietly looking at the top of her head. Finally, he said: "I was watching it all the way up from the station whenever I could get a glimpse of it." It was astonishing how quickly one could get back to the old level with Mig. It wasn't necessary to explain things.

"You didn't spot that it was new?"

"Should I have?"

Mig considered the matter for a moment. "No," she said tolerantly. "They made a good job of it. You'll learn."

"Whee!" Clinton indicated that he was hurt, but Mig only laughed, and he asked: "You still haven't said 'why?' "

"The Prof again." Mig's voice had a note of patient resignation that was completely false.

Clinton lifted a puzzled eyebrow. "Out of his country, isn't it?"

"The Dean's an old friend of his. When all this started"— she waved a grubby hand that took in comprehensively all the enormous work of restoration—"he asked the Prof to come down and give him a bit of advice. They were working on the north side then, between the Bell Tower and the nave. Then they decided to open up the foundations on this side—here." She indicated the hole and its extensions with another sweeping gesture. "We'd just come down to Bosham then. He told us we were wasting time doing whatever we were doing. He didn't even ask what it was—you know the Prof."

"And what was it?"

"Sailing in Chichester harbor, and it was fun. All he said was, 'You'd better come up here and watch as they turn the earth over.' "

"So you did?"

Mig shrugged. "You know the Prof." She repeated the phrase for emphasis.

"Why didn't he get university students? He usually does."

"He's a bit acid about university students at present— protests and long hair. He says they know too much."

Clinton almost squealed with delight. "What about *you?*"

"He said"—Mig's voice became impossibly dignified—"he said we were unorthodox but showed occasional gleams of intelligence."

"Wow!" Clinton called up an expression from the ancient past. It seemed the only one that suited. "And what has your occasional gleam of intelligence turned up—to date?"

Mig looked at him with a sort of stolid innocence a·ıd said nothing.

Clinton knew that look. He abandoned the direct attack at once. He could always work round to it obliquely later. Instead he asked: "Where's Peter?"

"Peter," said Mig precisely, "is with the father of the Master-Builder. He was summoned."

It was plain that she wasn't going to add anything to that either. Clinton watched her drawing in the exact position of the potsherd on the large-scale plan. She added depth and distance from the main foundation in small clear lettering, and then said frivolously: "Not that it matters a flip of a fish's tail, but you've got to do it for the Prof. He likes his drawings tidy. I said it was like a Christmas pudding. Schliemann himself couldn't make a connected story out of it." She hesitated for a moment and added with characteristic honesty: "It was the Prof who said that."

Clinton laughed outright before he asked: "Who's Schliemann?"

"You know—the man who found Troy—if it is Troy. That was the Prof too." Mig clearly was having a candid spell. It did not, of course, interfere with her passion for making other people work. Barely pausing, she added: "Come on. Get down to it! We're working back to the big block there." She indicated a badly eroded stone in the foundations of the wall of the retrochoir that just showed above the normal surface. This time Clinton knew better than to ask why.

They worked in a companionable silence, falling automatically into old routines. It was a whole year since they had last worked together, but it always happened this way with the three of them.

Suddenly Mig half turned, recognizing particular footsteps amongst the constant passage of feet along the alleys of the cloister. "Peter," she said confidently.

They watched her brother come through the Paradise Wicket. He had no air of triumph about him. As soon as he was close enough Mig called, her voice urgent: "Will he?"

Peter shook his head.

"Trouble?" demanded Mig.

Peter shook his head again. "No trouble," he said, a little doubtfully.

Peter waited a moment, trying to find the right words. "He's so old," he said at last. "I can't tell you how old he is, and his voice seems to come from—I don't know—from far away somewhere. It's quite clear. He says exactly what he means, nothing else. I thought it all out on the way . . ."

Mig interrupted him. "Did you get there on time?"

"I got there on time"—Peter made an irritable gesture—"and I told him exactly what we'd found . . ."

"I thought you weren't going to tell him until he agreed to help us," Mig interrupted for a second time.

Peter shook his head. "No. It didn't work that way. It couldn't, you see. He sits there quite still and you can see all the bones in his head, and you listen to his voice and there isn't anything you can do about it. No"—he shook his head as if there had been a third interruption—"I couldn't offer to make a trade or anything like that. It wasn't on. It just wasn't on. I know why the Dean was scared now."

"But what did he say?" Mig repeated it. "What *did* he say?"

"He said, 'How many of you know about this?' I said, you"

—he nodded at Mig—"and that Clint"—he nodded at the American boy—"would have arrived and I expected you would have told him by this time, and he said, 'American?' And I said, 'Yes,' and he said nothing for so long that I thought I'd put my foot in it somehow. And then he said, 'Ten-thirty tomorrow. Here. All three of you.'"

"And that was all?"

"That was all," said Peter, frowning. "I don't know. It seemed an awful lot while I was there but it doesn't seem much now." He made a helpless little gesture with his shoulders and the palms of his hands opened outward. "He does something to you."

"Actually, I haven't told Clint anything." Mig watched her brother.

"I don't suppose it matters anyway," he answered vaguely.

"All that marvelous self-restraint," said Mig regretfully, "wasted. Every drop of it!"

Clint, who had been looking from one to the other, asked mildly: "Right! Does anyone tell me anything now?"

"You've got to know sometime," began Peter. "We can make a start at least. Mig . . ."

"Parentals," interrupted Mig hurriedly. "Mother, anyway, and the Dean."

"It'll have to wait. Sorry!"

They climbed out of the hole as Mrs. Manson came toward them, joining Peter on the battered turf of the graveyard. Clinton went forward, all full of what he called his old-fashioned Southern courtesy.

Mrs. Manson said: "It's good to see you again, Clint. Dean, this is Clinton Hammond—Dean Luttrell."

The Dean held out his hand.

He then turned to Peter. "And how was Old Mr. Ramidge?" he asked casually. The Dean's intelligence network always provoked Peter's reluctant respect. He decided to try a frontal defense.

"You always know, sir."

The Dean laughed outright. "After all, it's my cathedral! How was he?"

"I don't know," said Peter with absolute honesty. "This isn't being rude, sir, but it was like listening to something very ancient—not a mummy, but an ancient statue—talking."

"There are times," said the Dean, with emphasis, "when he's as baleful as a mummy. Did he tell you what you wanted to know?"

Peter made a quick gesture of dissent. "Not a word. All he said was, 'Be here tomorrow at ten-thirty. All three of you.' "

Mrs. Manson looked at the Dean. "Ought they to be worrying the old man?"

"Worrying him!" answered the Dean. "He's much more likely to be worrying them." He looked keenly at Peter. "I'm not sure that he isn't."

Peter looked back at him. "He seems so frail, sir. Is he?"

"Frail? He's as tough as a ten-inch nail."

Mrs. Manson turned. "We've got to collect Clint's things from the station."

The Dean bowed gently, but before he moved he said: "If he knows what you want to know, he'll tell you if he likes you. Farm tractors wouldn't get it out of him otherwise. If he's told you to come again, at least he hasn't taken an instant dislike." He grinned at Peter with a half-malicious sympathy. "I've never discovered anything on earth that he does like except the view from the window of the room he lives in out over Chichester to the Channel past Selsey Bill."

Peter nodded, a worried look on his face. "Can I ask you one more question, sir?"

"You may."

The boy looked apprehensively at Clinton. "Has he got anything against Americans?"

The Dean caught Clinton's eye and grinned. "Inevitably,"
he said. "He's got something against every nation. You get him
to talk about the English. You'll see!"

Chapter THREE

"DO we tell him about Bozzum now or do we let him pick it up as he goes along?" asked Mig from the front seat next to her mother.

"Kinder to tell him now," said her brother.

"Don't believe everything they're going to hand out," said Mrs. Manson amiably.

"Quiet, Mother!" Mig sounded as if she were talking to a beloved pet. "First thing—Bozzum's different."

"I know," said Clinton distantly.

"How?"

"Wouldn't spell itself B-o-s-h-a-m if it wasn't."

"Love-fifteen," said Mrs. Manson.

"You can't tell." Mig's voice went up the scale. "The next town but one's spelt C-o-s-h-a-m and calls itself *Cosh* am."

"That's all right." Clinton yielded the point. "This is England."

"Love-thirty," said Mrs. Manson.

Peter decided to take a hand. "Historically it's pretty important."

"Two pictures of it in the Bayeux Tapestry"—Clinton was beginning to enjoy himself—"labeled *Bosham ecclesia.*"

"Forty-love," said Mrs. Manson, laughing.

"And Canute's palace was there and Harold left from the harbor to go to Normandy the time he was shipwrecked. That's what led to all the trouble."

"Game—and so far as I am concerned, set," said Mrs. Manson. "All you can do is offer him local gossip now. He's trumped all your aces."

"I do my homework," said Clinton with insufferable modesty.

Mig groaned. "I might have known! The church is still there and they're doing a dig this year on the palace site. We'll take you."

They turned off the road, ran fifty yards down a lane and turned in through a dogwood hedge. The cottage was long and low and thatched. There wasn't a right-angle anywhere. It looked warm and livable and the deep swag in the roof had an oddly human and dissolute air.

Clinton looked at it with awe. "It's for real!" he said, cramming a whole wealth of appreciation into the single syllable.

"Fifteenth century." Peter accepted the appreciation at its proper value. "And the Prof says that he thinks that three walls of the buildings at the back are Saxon. It's a wonderful place, Bosham. You never know what you'll turn up."

"The next thing you'll turn up is lunch." Mrs. Manson's tone was placid but positive. "Clint's probably hungry, I certainly am, and you always are. You can take him round and blind him with history afterwards."

"I doubt it," admitted Peter reluctantly.

On the low bridge over the mill leat Mig said: "The Quay Meadow. It's National Trust now."

Clinton had won enough points. He didn't even bother to say, "I know." Instead he asked: "Was this where Canute had his big tide-defying scene?"

The others accepted that he was serious. Peter made a small helpless gesture. "Nobody knows. Southampton claims it happened there. It could have happened at Selsey—the Saxon kings had a palace there too. But the Men of Bosham say that it was here, and we know his own palace was here and we're living here anyway." He hesitated for a moment. "Defying isn't the right word, though."

"I thought he was big-headed and . . ."

"That's what everybody says." Peter nodded earnestly. "It could have been the other way round though."

"How?" Clinton frowned.

"That he was sick of his courtiers' sucking up and telling him how wonderful he was and did it to show them up."

"Not what the books say." Clinton's voice was doubtful.

"He was a commonsense sort of character"—Peter's tone was obstinate—"and he'd lived here long enough to know what the tide can do. It's about half ebb now. Wait till it goes out and you'll see! I tried my theory last term in a history essay."

"Any joy?"

"Not a whoop. Old Carter's the stuffiest . . ."

Mig said: "Let's sit on the wall. We can talk there."

The harbor was almost incandescent in the afternoon sun. The light came blinding off the water and only the rich green trees of Chidham across the channel made a cool marginal shadow under the glare of the sky. The little clouds had vanished utterly. A blue-sailed Skipper-class dinghy and a red-sailed Skipper followed each other in a lazy intricate chase. Even the gulls were settled and somnolent along the wall.

"Heh!" said Clinton. "This is better than an apartment block in Rome on a hot afternoon." He paused to jeer frivolously at a gull as it took off from the wall. "Go sit some place else." His voice was entirely happy as he turned to Peter. "Come on! What gives?"

"We don't really know yet ourselves." Peter spoke with an uncomfortable honesty. "We've found something. Seventy years ago Old Mr. Ramidge found something. If we can put the two things together, they may tell us something else."

"Clear," said Clinton sarcastically; "clear as canned milk. You try, Mig. You aren't so shocking honest."

Mig looked at her brother and back at Clinton. "We've found a block of stone."

"Mig found it," said her brother hurriedly.

"You and your conscience shut up!" snapped Clinton. "Go on, Mig!"

"I spotted some deep scratches on it so we cleaned it up a bit and they seemed to make sense."

"As how?"

"As a map. Only the block was broken and they ended in midair."

"Map of what?"

"The coast."

"Here?"

"No—from about Pagham to Selsey Bill."

"How d'you know?"

"We don't. But up here near the top the coastline—if it is the coastline—runs inland and the shape's like the shape of Pagham Harbor. Two deep creeks to the north and a wide one to the southwest, and a narrow entrance. Just about what Pagham Harbor must have been before they tried to block it up."

"Anything else?"

"Three crosses cut into the stone." Mig's voice had a note of triumph. "One where St. Wilfred's chapel ought to be if Pagham Harbor's Pagham Harbor. One at Pagham itself where St. Thomas à Becket's church is . . ."

Obediently Peter knelt down and began to trace a line in the dust. "Bognor up here"—he indicated an area beyond the beginning of the line—"and this is what we think is Pagham Harbor." He sketched in a shape with two deep indentations to the north, a third trending to the southwest and a firm curve back to the eastward. He marked a narrow entrance channel, doubled the line back and drew it in firmly for about eight inches. "Then it swings round to the west, runs more or less straight for a bit, and then heads northwest and off the stone."

"And what else?"

"Dunno." Peter's worried frown had come back. "Point where it turns west"—he put the twig with which he had made the scratches at the angle of the line—"is way south of Selsey Bill—or at any rate of where Selsey Bill is nowadays. Present coastline's about here." He drew in a second line.

"Meaning?"

"Erosion," Peter explained hurriedly. "Coast's been washing away at the Bill for a thousand years—more!"

"How big are these scratches?"

" 'Bout this size," Peter answered. "They're grooves, really."

"Big stone!"

"Half a big stone," Mig corrected him.

Peter drew in another line above the Pagham inlet. "This is the edge of the break."

"And the third cross?" Clinton missed little.

"Here." Peter made a firm mark just above the lower line; it was twice the size of the others.

"That's in the sea now, if your lines are right!"

Peter nodded dumbly.

"All right. Give!"

Mig took up the running. "It's like the other two crosses only bigger. Much bigger. If *they* mark churches—and we're certain they do—*it* marks a bigger church!" Her voice was completely positive.

"And it's in the sea?" Clinton's tone was skeptical.

"That's right."

"Meaning?"

"It may"—Peter was infinitely cautious—"it just *may* mark the position of the old cathedral."

"What old cathedral, for Pete's sake?"

"The first one. The one that St. Wilfred founded—long before Chichester."

"But not *at* Chichester?"

"No, at Selsey."

Clinton ran his hands through his hair. "I know I'm stupid, but does anybody want to explain?"

"It's easy." Mig's voice was blithe. "Wilfred was wrecked somewhere about here. It could have been on the Bill. He was coming back from France—from Paris. So he built a cathedral. They did in those days."

"And the sea came in and drowned it?"

"Oh, no!" Mig shook her head. "That was a long time afterwards."

"Why's the new cathedral at Chichester then?"

"William the Conqueror," Mig said, as if everybody ought to know.

"One thing you can bet on with the English," Clinton snapped, "sooner or later they all come back to William the Conqueror. What's he got to do with it?"

"He"—she hesitated and then went on—"he rationalized the English cathedrals." It was a new word and she was proud of it. "He made them shift from villages and small towns to the big towns where there was population enough to fill 'em and he could keep an eye on the bishops."

"And there wasn't a town at Selsey?"

"There were two towns but they weren't more than big villages." Mig refused to try to make things easier. "Norton, where the church is on Pagham Harbor, and Sutton, on the Bill, but Saxon Sutton must have disappeared five hundred years ago. They weren't either of them big enough for a cathedral—not even both together. Chichester had been Roman and it was Saxon. It was quite a place, even then. There was a Saxon church there too."

"I think I've got it." Clinton smoothed down his hair. "So they shifted the one at Selsey and put it up at Chichester?"

Peter came back into the conversation. "I expect they shifted what they could. It wouldn't have been much. There's practically no Saxon work at Chi, except under the north transept ... and—" He cut himself off abruptly.

"And what?"

Mig interrupted her brother, looking anxiously at the American boy. "It isn't a secret or anything, Clint. It's just that we want you to see what it is for yourself first. Telling you might spoil it. 'Tisn't easy to describe. We'll show you it as soon as we get back to Chi. Mother'll be ready"—she looked at her wristwatch—"in twenty minutes."

"You two are the worst . . ." Clinton heaved his shoulders up to his ears. "I just don't know! Tell me just—"

"You must preserve your soul in patience." Mig made her voice infuriatingly prim. "You know you'll have to anyway. You might twist my arm or Peter's if we were alone but not with both of us together."

Clinton admitted defeat. He said acidly: "State of extreme tension"; was silent for half a minute, and then added softly, "now tell me the rest!"

"What rest?" Peter was looking anxious again.

"Your hundred-year egg or whatever he is. Where does he fit in?"

"Old Mr. Ramidge! I forgot about him. Stupid! Old Mr. Ramidge found the other half of the stone, sixty—seventy years ago."

"Did he spot what it was?"

"He guessed, I think. Don't know that he was ever quite sure. He was on the works staff then. Afterwards he was the Master-Builder's assistant, after that he was the Master-Builder himself."

"Why didn't he do anything about it, then?"

"He did. He searched and searched." Mig's voice was curiously understanding. "No luck—ever. He couldn't find it. He told his son about it though, when he had to retire. But he never told him where his own piece was."

"Would his son have recognized it if he saw it?"

"Of course!"

"How?"

"It's a special kind of limestone. Comes from Purbeck. People used to think it was Caen stone, but it's not."

"Isn't there any more of it in the cathedral?"

"A bit," answered Peter reluctantly.

"Such as?"

"We'll show you," Mig put in indirectly, coming to Peter's help.

"Forgot to bring my thumbscrews with me." Clinton clicked his tongue, despairingly sarcastic. "Remind me to remember next time."

Peter refused to be drawn. Instead he stood up and said with authority: "Let's go!"

Getting up, they frightened five more gulls. Children raced along the wall, frightening the rest. The sky was suddenly full of swirling black and white shapes.

There were seven people on the little quay, staring down at the water below them after the manner of people on quay-sides. Two boys sat on the edge, swinging their legs. The mast of a dinghy—the boat itself invisible—jerked and swayed as her crew readied her for hoisting sail. At the far end of the quay an outboard motor roared into life and the speedboat to which it was attached appeared dramatically, poised on the tumbled water of its wake. It zigzagged wildly through the forest of anchored yachts.

The three turned left toward the watermill and crossed the little race as it fell away from the black timber of the wheel channel. The tide was coming in fast. In places water crept tentatively toward the tarmac of the lower road.

Clinton regarded it with interest. "Ever come right over?"

"At high water of spring tides, always."

"Automobiles?"

"They get caught." Mig laughed lightheartedly. "It's one of the local sports and pastimes. People come from miles around to see it. *They* park in the village parking lot."

"Doesn't anybody warn strangers?"

"There are warning notices." Mig made a face at him. "You know what people are."

"Deep?"

"Up to a car roof with a special tide. Look at the walls under the houses."

"Then there *is* something worse than traffic wardens! Nobody'll believe this in Washington."

"Stuffy!" Mig mocked him openly. "If they won't read the notices. . . . They all went to school."

"And what's that got to do with it?"

"Must have learnt about Canute."

Clinton threw away stuffiness and began to laugh. They were still laughing when Mrs. Manson and the station wagon came into sight.

Chapter FOUR

CLINTON stared at the immense complexity of scaffolding and struts and girders that propped up the north transept of the cathedral. "Nobody told me it was as bad as this. How come?"

"It's old." Peter ticked off the reasons on his fingers. "Best part of a thousand years. It didn't have proper foundations in the first place. It had two big fires early on and they re-used stone that had perished through the heat when they rebuilt. So . . ." He gestured toward the reconstruction.

"That doesn't look too good, either." Clinton turned toward the belfry.

"My Bell Tower," said Mig fondly. "Most of that's on the outside. Ordinary weathering. It'll have to be done sometime though. That's Caen stone, by the way."

"Why your Bell Tower?"

"I love it." Mig made a little movement of her hands as if she were stroking it. "It's the only separate one left in England —in the cathedrals, that is. That's one reason, the other is that it's a joke."

"What d'you mean—joke?"

"There was a law about Caen stone, sort of sumptuary law. Only the king and the top clergy were allowed to import it— for cathedrals and abbeys and minsters and such . . ."

"And?"

"Local legend says there was a new-rich landowner hereabouts in the fifteenth century and he tried to smuggle in a cargo of Caen stone to build a better house than anybody else's and they ganged up on him."

"What happened?"

"The king—must have been Edward IV or somebody—grabbed the cargo and passed it on to the bishop, and the bishop built the belfry." Mig paused for a little, humorously contemplating the indignation of the landowner. "He must have been hopping mad every time he heard the bells," she said happily.

The three drifted slowly toward the west doorway.

"I thought your father took you to most of the cathedrals. Didn't he ever bring you here?"

"Canterbury, Winchester, Salisbury, and Exeter in the south here, but for some reason he missed out on Chichester. Don't know why."

"It's good," said Mig proprietorially. She had a tendency to own anything that filled her with enthusiasm.

The west door was open as they went in out of the blaze of the afternoon, the great Norman nave was by contrast dark and cavernous. Across its eastern end above the steps that led to the choir the three superb arches of the Arundel screen picked up a silver light from the afternoon windows. Through the arches was a riot of scarlet and flame color, of blue and green and gold.

Clinton stood motionless inside the doorway. "What," he asked, "is that?"

Mig, watching the direction of his eyes, guessed and said: "The Piper tapestries. We rather like it from here. We can take it about halfway up the nave. We're not sure after that, we think it's a bit psychedelic."

Clinton considered it for a little. "Could be," he said at length. "Where do we go?"

They went across to the south aisle and walked slowly up

the narrow and delicate beauty of its recessions. Clinton was like a young hound, questing. The other two knew his eager interest in the great churches. Nothing was said. They let him quest.

Three steps led up to the south choir aisle. They went up them, crossed the south transept and came to the bays of the presbytery. They had let Clinton move ahead. He stopped abruptly now of his own accord. Behind him Peter and Mig waited.

After a long silence he asked, wonderingly: "Is it something to do with this?"

Peter nodded. "Mig said you'd know as soon as you saw it."

"I hoped," said Mig.

"It's one of the Lazarus panels, isn't it?" Clinton disregarded them both. "I'd forgotten even that they were at Chichester. My pop told me about them then. He said that they were the best medieval sculptures in England. What in creation have they got to do with your map?"

"The stone's the same," said Peter, a shade doggedly. "There isn't another piece of it in the cathedral that we know of—not anywhere. The borders match. They're the same width, the same shape. I know that these were built up"—he pointed at the panel—"out of small blocks and then carved, and our block was one piece, but it was only half the width of a panel. And we think it could have been an end piece, a sort of frame holding them together, or perhaps there were plain pieces between each pair of panels."

"And we believe they came from Selsey—from the old cathedral." Mig's voice was superbly confident.

"That'd make them Saxon?"

"It would." Peter nodded. His uncomfortable honesty took over again. "A lot of people say they're Norman. Dr. Zarnecki says they're not earlier than 1125."

"Who's Dr. Zarnecki?"

Peter shrugged his shoulders. "Search me! The Prof says they're much earlier. He's certain they're Saxon. And we"—Peter was totally loyal—"we back the Prof."

"Where's the other one, the—the Bethany panel?"

Mig pointed to a cased-in mass that projected from the obviously temporary screen of fiberboard that blocked off the end of the aisle. There was a wide opening in the screen like an observation window in a building site. "It's boxed in for now."

"Why?"

"Come and see." Mig went forward and put her arms on the ledge of the opening. "That!" she said, pointing downward.

In a cavernous excavation below the floor level of the aisle was an astonishing confusion of sandbags and broken stone, of bricks, black earth, ragged foundation, new concrete and reinforcing steel. In the middle of it, lit by a powerful light, a mosaic pavement glowed, delicate, admirably designed, and where it had not been broken up when the first work on the cathedral started, in singular condition.

"The whole cathedral's built on Roman houses. Town houses. If that's anything to go by"—she pointed at the mosaic again—"rich houses." She looked down fondly into the ordered chaos of the excavation. "Lovely, isn't it? The Prof's coming down for another look at it tomorrow before they start on the retaining walls. We'll have about two hours to talk him into helping us."

Again Clinton seemed to ignore her. "I'm beginning to get it—I think. You reckon that your stone was a part of the screen or whatever it was that these were in, and that because they used it for the map, that the map has to do with them."

"Something like that." Peter turned uneasily. "We can't be

certain—yet. But it could have been made to show where they came from. We're absolutely certain that it was made to show where the old cathedral was. If we could find it—find the foundations, because that's all that could be left—or even enough squared stone to prove that it had been there—it would be a big thing—an important thing." His voice was almost pleading.

Clinton turned away from him, back to the beauty of the panel, staring at the splendid formal figures of the scene. Christ's hand was raised commandingly above Lazarus, apostles surrounded him. Martha and Mary watched naïvely astonished. The carving had a compelling simplicity, a great power.

"They were found behind the choir stalls," explained Peter, "somewhere back in the 1820's. Nobody seems to know who put them there or why, but the stalls were built somewhere about 1330, so they must have been hidden the best part of five hundred years."

Mig joined in. "Everybody argues about how old they are— nobody seems to bother about where they came from. There's a legend—but you can't go by legend."

Peter took it up again. "It says there were three of them once, or perhaps five even—there's a bit of another one in the Library—and that they were carved for Wilfred's cathedral and brought here for the new building."

"And Ralph of Luffa built a sort of screen—"

"A reredos."

"Behind the high altar anyway, and that they were damaged in the fire. There was an apse at this end before the fire, but when Bishop Seffrid rebuilt it after the fire he made it square. We'll show you afterwards."

"And we think they must have built these into the walls of the choir, not wanting to destroy them."

"Not daring to," said Mig.

"And the others—if there are others?" Clinton came straight to the point.

"We don't know." Peter spoke with his usual blunt honesty. "They could have been ruined absolutely in the fire—if they were ever brought here, that is—or they could have been left in the old cathedral."

"Under water?"

"Under water *now* anyway," agreed Peter.

"Which explains scuba suits."

"It does. What d'you think?" asked Mig anxiously.

"Can you plot the position of a cathedral from scratches on a stone?"

Once more Peter was painfully honest. "I don't know if we can—yet. Perhaps when we've seen Old Mr. Ramidge's half of it. Even then it isn't going to be easy. 'Tisn't like a modern map. No scale, no compass bearings. Masses of distortion."

"Can I see your half?"

"No." Peter's voice was awkward.

"Why?"

"We buried it again," said Mig sweetly. "Use your loaf!"

Chapter FIVE

"HELP yourself," said Mig hospitably. She waved half a cold sausage in the air in a gesture that was at once a greeting and an invitation. "You'll find a dish of 'em in the refrigerator, and milk. You can't have a Coke as early as this in the morning; it would be bad for your digestion."

"Won't your mother—?"

"Not until eight," Mig answered. "As long as we're out by eight. She's likely to throw things if we hang around after that. Depends on what sort of a night she's had," she added tolerantly.

Clinton burrowed into the refrigerator. His voice reverberated from the back of it. "Where's Pete?"

"Getting the charts and things." Mig flourished the sausage again. "He's got a thing about secrecy."

Peter's voice said through the open door: "And you talk too much. Somebody's got to balance it. 'Lo, Clint! Let's look at the Admiralty Chart first. It gives you the general idea." He slipped the cap off the cylinder and extracted the sheet. The legend said: ENGLAND—SOUTH COAST. Christchurch to Owers. He unrolled it on the table, flattened it and put a book at each end. "Selsey Bill." He put his finger on the extreme right of the chart. The low, flat headland jutted out from the main coastal plain. To the east of the coastline there was a neat, bold dotted line in red. Peter moved his finger. "Pagham Harbor," he said, as it stopped in the new position.

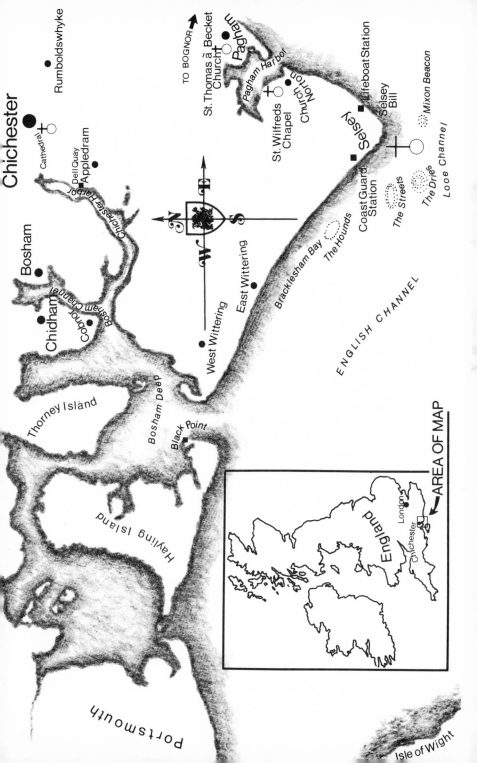

He lifted his finger again and traced a rough square. "That's the area that the map on this bit of the stone covers. The break is in the middle of Bracklesham Bay, as far as we can judge." His fingers traced the line of the firm red dots.

Clinton grunted. "The rubbing—show me the rubbing!"

"He's impatient," Mig mocked the boy.

"I reckon I'm entitled." Clinton stared at her. "Anybody trying to get a couple of straight facts out of you two—" He left the sentence unfinished.

Peter felt in the cylinder again, got the corner of a big sheet of drawing paper between his first two fingers, and eased it out. He put it down on top of the chart, shifted one of the books to weight it, and flattened it across the table. Mig caught and held the far end.

" 'Tisn't perfect. We had to work pretty darn fast." Mig's voice was explanatory rather than apologetic. "There were people about most of the time."

"It must have been some kind of panel," Peter explained. "There's this flat molding, like a sort of frame, round three sides of it."

"That's what made me look at it," interjected Mig.

Peter traced the edges of the molding with his fingers. "Absolutely flat inside the frame. The break's across here." His finger ran along the top of the rubbing.

It was slightly irregular, ragged compared with the careful mason's work of the rest of the block. Allowing for weathering, the edges were astonishingly distinct. The insides of the moldings had come out sharply black in the rubbing, and over the smoothness of the interior surface the grooves were completely clear, heavily marked in charcoal. Even at this first glance Clinton could see that they were artificial and deliberate.

Peter put his finger to the point where the line began. "Coast comes sharply to the south'ard after Bognor. Runs quite clean to the north spit at Pagham Harbor entrance and cuts back much as it does now. There's a lot of distortion in the bight to the west of Pagham here, but it's probably changed a bit since then. I couldn't draw it properly yesterday."

"The chart," demanded Clinton. "Let's see the chart!"

Mig passed him a sheet with a clear and simple sketch map of the area. "That's from *Local Knowledge*. It's easier to follow."

"Good!" Peter nodded approvingly. "It comes round just a bit west of where it ought to and you've got the little bay up to Danesacre here. 'Tisn't as deep as this really. Then it goes down where it ought to go down—but ever so much wider than it is now—to the southwest." He hesitated and went on, just a little like a teacher of geography: "Selsey was still almost an island then. Even now you can cross that area by the bridge at the Ferry House, and it still runs southwest right down to the coast—almost to the beach. It bends back there where the shingle in Bracklesham Bay blocked it off. Ethelwalch—he was the King of the South Saxons—gave Wilfred a grant of land. There's a description of it somewhere—Venerable Bede, I think—which says: 'the land of eighty-seven families in Selaesue . . . the island of the Sea-Calf.' "

"Then it comes back to the sea again." Clinton was completely absorbed now, his eyes switching restlessly back and forth from the rubbing to the chart in his hand.

The depth of the cut on the stone was bolder here than anywhere except toward the extreme south. "I think it was this bit that we recognized first." Peter was allowing himself to become excited. "It's just like it is now. We told you about St. Wilfred's chapel yesterday, there's the cross." He put his fingernail below the small symbol. "It shows clearer on this than it does on the stone, but I think it's just a trick of the light. See what I meant yesterday? If this *is* Pagham Harbor,

the cross has got to be Wilfred's chapel and the second cross
has got to be St. Thomas à Becket on the Bognor side."

"It figures." Clinton accepted the point. "And this?" His
finger followed the red line on the chart.

"The south spit—it's sand, and it shifts. It was farther out
then. They tried to reclaim the harbor once. *Their* line comes
south from there, well out from the line of the coast today.
This is as near as we can plot it. We've tried it every way we
could. The dotted red line runs on the edge of the one-fathom
line straight down toward the Mixon reef. It swings west before
it reaches the Mixon though—'bout half a mile offshore."

Clinton's eye studied the gap and took in the scale of the
chart. "The reef itself's a mile off?"

"All of that," agreed Peter. "Land must have been slashed
back a long way already when this was drawn."

"And you reckon the old cathedral was . . . ?"

"Where I showed you yesterday—here!" Peter rested the
point of his finger delicately on the third cross, sharp and
unmistakable athwart the red dots of the line that marked
the ancient limits of the tide.

Mig whispered eagerly: "It's got to be! It's got to be!"

Clinton disregarded her. His face was almost buried in the
Admiralty chart again. "Rock." He lifted up one eyebrow and
squinted across at Peter.

"I think so," said Peter.

"And sand?"

"It would be."

"Not a reef anyway." Clinton seemed to satisfy himself. He
was silent for a long time, studying the small patch of water,
pale blue on the chart inside the three-fathom mark. Finally
he straightened and said, enigmatically: "Could be."

Mig, unable to restrain herself any longer, asked: "D'you
think there's a chance?"

"How would I know?" Clinton looked at her severely. "It's guesswork so far, isn't it? We've got to see the rest of the map and we've got to work out the distances, and then we've got to decide where we think it is. We can't even begin to start till after that."

Mig smiled to herself. He was saying "we," not "you." She knew her Clint.

Again there was a long silence while he studied the chart. Finally he lifted up one of the weights, let the rubbing roll up, and put it on one side. "All this sheltered water," he said at length, staring at the chart, "and you've got to pick the most exposed point of land for fifteen miles in any direction: You'd *do* that, wouldn't you?" He glowered at Mig.

"St. Wilfred did it," said Mig cheerfully. "He was wrecked here—not me."

"What's it like off the Bill?" Clinton stared at Peter.

"When it's fine, it's fine. When it blows from the east or from the south . . ." He left everything to Clinton's imagination. Then, apparently worried about upsetting him, he added: "The lobstermen seem to make out all right. Still quite a few of them at Selsey."

"Know any?"

"We've talked to one or two, that's all." Mig looked thoughtful.

"Then we've got to get to know 'em, haven't we? There'll be a bit of shelter from the Isle of Wight with a westerly wind, but not that much—not for a small boat. What about the tides?"

"Strong," said Peter frankly. "You'll find a bit about it in *Local Knowledge.* Two and a half knots at the height of the ebb in The Looe Channel; three tides meet there—there's more than a bit of a race!"

"Show!"

Peter put his finger on the chart. "In the gut between the Boulder Bank and The Dries."

"That's all of a mile farther out," said Clinton. "It oughtn't to be as bad in the shallows."

"What shallows?" Mrs. Manson had come in through the door behind them.

As Clinton politely said: "Good morning, Mrs. Manson. I hope you slept well," Mig, keeping her voice low and level, said: "The shallows off Selsey Bill."

Mrs. Manson turned to the kitchen table. "Off with that lot or you don't get any breakfast!"

Mig hugged herself gleefully. It might be necessary to say to her mother at some future date: "Oh, but I *told* you we were going to work in the shallows off Selsey Bill. Don't you remember that morning when we had the charts all over the kitchen table?" It was useful to have something in reserve.

"You wouldn't like to come up with us and meet him?" Peter's voice was almost wheedling.

His mother was completely positive. "You fight your own wars! You can't say nobody's told you about him. Out you go! I'm hardhearted this morning."

"It's quite a long way up the drive."

"The exercise will do you good." Mrs. Manson used one of the oldest of parental responses. "You've got plenty of time in hand. If you miss the bus back, walk!"

Mig said: "The trouble with you is that you haven't any maternal sympathy."

"Never on a shopping morning," Mrs. Manson answered tartly. "Get along with you—and don't worry Old Mr. Ramidge!"

"Us?" Her son turned up his eyes. "Worry *him*!"

Mrs. Manson let in the clutch and laughed.

They walked up the drive slowly, killing time. The house almost overhung the top part of it. The big window that formed the end of Old Mr. Ramidge's room was open and, as Peter gestured up to it, they became silent.

When she thought they were out of earshot again Mig asked: "D'you think he heard us?"

"You getting scared too?" It was more a statement than a question.

"I've got." Mig nodded.

"Can't understand you two." Clinton looked at them disparagingly. "He's got the stuffing beat out of you before you've got to the door."

"You wait!" Peter shook his head. "I don't know how he does it. I've been scared since we came in at the gate."

"All right! He's an old buzzard." Clinton shook his head. "So what? You can run faster than him."

"Fly faster," suggested Mig.

"He *is* a bit like a vulture," conceded Peter, "sitting there all hunched up, waiting."

"For what?" asked Clinton derisively.

"Us!" said Mig, and they began to laugh together, keeping their laughter quiet.

Peter put his finger apprehensively on the bell push.

The elderly woman who opened the door was a stranger, but it was evident that she knew about them. She said, almost reproachfully: "You weren't to be here till ten-thirty."

Involuntarily Peter looked at his watch. It was twenty-seven minutes past the hour. Involuntarily he said: "I'm sorry."

"You'd best sit down here," muttered the woman gently, and went out, closing the door of the hall behind her.

Mig whispered: "She's as scared as we are."

Peter took out his handkerchief and mopped his face. Clinton watched them both with a glint in his eye.

At exactly ten-twenty-nine the door opened again, and the woman said: "This way," and opened a door that led into the long central room of the house, the room with the window. Old Mr. Ramidge was sitting in his wheelchair precisely as Peter had described him, exactly in the middle of the sweep of the window, exactly far enough back to be clear of any drafts, exactly upright but with his shoulders a little hunched and yet, Mig thought, he's not like a vulture—not a bit like one.

She walked straight to the front of his chair, turned and said quietly: "Good morning, Mr. Ramidge." She had intended to make a little speech, thanking him for letting them come, but instead she felt herself quite helplessly saying: "I think I would be happy if I were old and I had a view like this." She smiled. The brief moment was utterly natural.

The voice was even more remarkable than Peter's description of it. It was entirely clear but it was only a whisper, a thread of sound. Mr. Ramidge said: "It is a long time since anyone believed that I was happy." There was a moment of silence, than the rustle of sound came again. "You may be right. You are Miss Manson." Again there was a silence and then, as if he were yielding something important: "Mig Manson. I think I expected you to be different."

Peter came forward. He said quietly—they were all subdued: "Good morning, sir. We brought Clint Hammond with us. I think you wanted to see him too."

"I did."

This time the old man was quiet for so long that Peter began to search his mind for a new opening.

Mig broke the silence without difficulty. She asked: "May I look at your view? Please!" and turned and stood at the edge of the wide opening. "Selsey Bill," she said, picking out the landmarks, "Bembridge and the Island, and a big tanker going up to Fawley, and a frigate—two frigates—and all the flats and all the harbors and Chichester spire." She turned back to the old man. "Does it change quickly?"

"Very quickly." The old man seemed to have attuned himself to the working of her mind at once. "One small cloud across the sun will change it, or the wind on the water."

Peter and Clinton listened to the two of them, amazed.

"And birds?" asked Mig. "You have a bird table."

"They come in to me sometimes—tits and chaffinches, and robins in winter."

She sat down quite unselfconsciously on a chair close to him. "There's nothing near enough to spoil it."

"Nothing." The thin, remote voice seemed to brush away anything in the world that was unpleasant.

Again there was a silence, but at least to Mig there was absolutely nothing threatening in the silence now. She waited contentedly.

Old Mr. Ramidge turned his head so suddenly that there was almost an effect of shock. His distant, heavy-lidded eyes found Peter's face but his voice was still directed to Mig. He asked: "Your brother is"—he considered his choice of words carefully—"trustworthy?" There was no shadow of offense in the question.

Mig accepted it and answered it instantly. "Yes, Mr. Ramidge."

"Thank you," said the rustling voice, courteously. "I judged that yesterday." The head turned very slightly, this time to take in Clinton. "I had a friend, an American like you. It was during the First World War. There was something about a girl in France. I wondered if it ought to make a difference, but I thought about it carefully yesterday and I've forgotten it." Without altering his tone, he went on, this time to Peter: "You found your half of the stone in Paradise. It would be between the third buttress and the cloister wall?"

Peter said automatically—the voice seemed to draw its

answers regardless of anybody else's will: "You're right, sir."

"Now," said Old Mr. Ramidge, "you have nothing left to bargain with, you see." For the first time his voice held a touch of his celebrated malignancy.

Peter nodded. "I know, sir. But I couldn't refuse, could I? Can I ask you how you knew?"

There was the very faint ghost of a chuckle. "I asked my son where you'd been digging. He said between the last buttress and the cloister and that you had packed the earth back—carefully, he said."

Mig laughed outright. "And we were thinking we'd been terribly clever!"

Again there was a ghost of a chuckle and again silence. Finally the voice said, detached and precise: "My half is set in the ledge of the lancet window in the gable of the chapel of St. Mary Magdalene."

"The chapel with the Sutherland picture?" Peter murmured.

Old Mr. Ramidge nodded contentedly. "It's high. You'll need a long ladder."

"May we ask the Dean's permission to see it, sir?"

Again came the ghostly chuckle. "You'll have to do just as I did."

"What was that, sir?"

"Cleanse it," said Mr. Ramidge. "There'll be seventy years of new pigeon droppings since I was there. You'll have to shift it and wash it down before you'll see anything at all. I had to. There was seven hundred years of it then."

"How did you find it?" Mig looked at him, fascinated.

"I was meant to be examining the window stonework for cracks and I said it was clear, and the Master-Builder saw the pigeon droppings. I had to stay on and clean it."

"And you found?" Mig was not even hesitating now about questions.

The old man's head turned slowly toward her. There was a glint in the heavy eyes. "Scratches," said Mr. Ramidge. Again there was one of his silences.

Oddly they were none of them worried about the silences now. They waited in patience.

Mr. Ramidge seemed to have made up his mind. "You have of course made a drawing of your stone?"

Mig answered: "Better than that—we made a rubbing."

Mr. Ramidge did not even look at her as he said: "Naturally," and she was left puzzled.

"We've brought it with us," said Peter.

"Naturally," Mr. Ramidge repeated.

Peter grinned as he went out of the room to the hall and picked up his cyclinder. He was still grinning when he came back. He was beginning to understand Old Mr. Ramidge and the understanding was comforting. At ninety-two he was entitled to like his own way. The roll caught for a moment, freed itself and slid out. Mig took the edge of it and they unrolled it and held it, like a banner, in front of the old man.

For the first time he made a real movement. There was an instant, almost frightening eagerness as he leant forward and peered at the soft gray surface of the rubbing. Mig, watching his eyes, saw a quick certainty in their motion as they examined the complex indentation of Pagham Harbor and went from it straight down to the deep-cut cross that marked the old cathedral.

"Aaah," said Old Mr. Ramidge, and the monosyllable was like a long sigh. "After seventy years . . ."

Chapter SIX

"I also made a rubbing."

To Mig the old man's voice seemed stronger, more decisive. His whole bearing had changed. When she tried to explain it afterwards, she said: "I thought his head looked firmer on his neck."

"The fixatives were not as good in my day. It has faded—died out—but it will serve." He lifted his left hand and made a commanding gesture. "The second shelf from the floor in the press against the far wall."

"Sir," said Peter, and scurried down toward the end of the room.

"Between sheets of gray drawing paper. Sealed." The whispering voice was incisive. "Bring it!"

Peter found it almost at once and brought it back to the wheelchair.

"Open it!" said Mr. Ramidge.

Cautiously Peter opened the seals. As the old man had said, the paper was faded and brown and very old, and he extracted it with enormous care. Clinton moved for the first time, fascinated, and helped him.

Without any asking, Mig held up her own rubbing again, and Peter and Clinton matched the edges of the fracture, old and new, deftly together.

"Aaah!" said Old Mr. Ramidge.

Despite the age of the rubbing, there was never even a

moment of doubt. It was entirely clear that this was copied from the other half of their block of stone. The inside edges of the flat surfaces which framed it were identical with those of their own section. The edges of the break matched. The crosses were cut to precisely the same pattern—a large one at the top of the rubbing, a smaller cross to the southwest of it, another to the southeast. The larger one stood in the southwest angle of the intersection of two long, clear grooves, one of which ran east and west across the block roughly parallel to and just below the top of the frame. The other ran from north to south over the intersection and almost straight down the middle of the panel.

"What were these?" Peter's voice was enormously excited.

"The roads that meet at the Cross." Old Mr. Ramidge's tone was completely confident.

"And this?" Mig's finger touched a narrow irregular loop on the left-hand side of the panel that curved to the north until it almost reached the east-west road.

"Top of the Chichester channel," whispered the old man. "Coming up at Dell Quay—it has to be. The roads are as they are today. Plainly the cross is the cathedral . . ."

"Did you know at once it was a map, sir?"

"Not at once. Not at once—not for—I think—three years. Then I found a map at Winchester—in the cathedral library it was—a late map, fifteenth century at the earliest—very simple. It showed the southern coastline—the Solent—Portsmouth—Hayling Island. Chichester was marked with just such a cross and the parish churches. It came to me then." The voice was quieter than ever. It paused: then Mr. Ramidge said with a quiet finality: "Mrs. Miles will no doubt have some refreshment for you."

Peter said: "It's very good of you, sir," and shepherded the other two toward the door.

They left the rubbings carefully on the table.

"You've kept him wonderful quiet," said Mrs. Miles, pushing a plate of hot scones toward Clinton. "I wouldn't ever've believed it. Not once his bell, not once!"

Mig asked cheerfully: "Is he difficult sometimes?"

"Nearer to impossible." Mrs. Miles spoke slowly and carefully. "Nearer to impossible. 'Nother cup?" She was showing her gratitude in the appropriate manner.

Mig passed her cup across. As Mrs. Miles began to pour the tea, there was a clangor in the kitchen.

"Spoke too soon," said Mrs. Miles resignedly. "Spoke altogether too soon." She put the teapot down and added: "Help yourself, dearie," and went toward the big room.

The three relaxed as she went out.

"Done it!" said Peter. "No doubt now—not a shadow."

"You're sure?"

"Absolutely. It couldn't be anything else. We can get new measurements from *his* churches and check with our own. They won't be accurate, but they'll help if we strike an average."

Clinton asked: "Will he want us again?"

Peter shrugged. "Mrs. Miles will tell us."

They helped themselves to another scone apiece. Clinton had finished his and a sandwich as well before Mrs. Miles came back.

She beamed on them from the door. "Done him a whole world of good, you have!" She allowed a small note of criticism to enter her voice. "I didn't think it likely when you went in. Rare old devil he can be. Times."

"Did he say anything?" asked Mig.

"He said to tell you he'd send for you, and he told me to bring this out." She held up the metal cylinder.

Peter took it from her and looked inside. "And the rubbing?"

"Them two big sheets on the table?" asked Mrs. Miles.

"That's right."

"He said to leave them—said it quite clear. So I left them."

"The old so-and-so!" exclaimed Peter ruefully. "Now he's got both. D'you think I could go back in and ask him, Mrs. Miles?"

"No," said Mrs. Miles. "He's asleep. Went right off after, the way he does."

"We'll have to make our own rubbing then," declared Peter. "Means cleaning off seventy years of pigeon!"

Mig began to laugh. "I think he meant that."

Young Mr. Ramidge looked at them with something approaching awe. "He never shouted? He didn't swear? He never rang Mrs. Miles's bell? He didn't send you out of the room?"

"Except when he sent us out to get something to eat," said Mig. "I don't believe he ever shouts. He's a darling!"

Young Mr. Ramidge looked at her with his head on one side. "You're probably the first girl who's said that of him for half a century." He considered his words for a moment and added: "He doesn't really shout. It's just that when he's angry it seems like shouting. Did he tell you what you wanted to know?"

"We saw the rubbing that he made," Peter said simply.

"You did, did you?" The Master-Builder's voice was respectful. "I've only seen it twice. Where is it?"

"With *our* rubbing—on *his* table," admitted Peter reluctantly. "I think he organized us into leaving it."

"You can bet on that!" Young Mr. Ramidge's voice was decided. "What I meant was: did he tell you how to find his stone?"

"It's set in the ledge of the lancet in the gable of the chapel of St. Mary Magdalene."

"Outside or inside?"

"Outside."

"I had a look at the lancet"—Mr. Ramidge thought for a puzzled moment—"must have been the year before last." He shook his head firmly.

"He says it'll be covered with seventy years of pigeon droppings."

"Aaah!" Young Mr. Ramidge's voice was for a moment like an amplified version of his father's. "I never thought of that."

"May we clean it and make a rubbing?" Peter looked beseechingly at the Master-Builder.

"The Dean . . ."

"Is at a conference at Lambeth," put in Mig hurriedly. "He won't be back until Friday, and we can't wait, Mr. Ramidge! We just can't!" She watched his face anxiously and added: "Besides—your father . . ."

The Master-Builder remembered his father and yielded. "You'll need a long ladder. Ask Mr. Parry; he'll know what to use. Don't scrape—wash it! And make your rubbing when it's dry."

Mig said gratefully: "You're almost as nice as your father."

Young Mr. Ramidge laughed—and then looked doubtful.

It took the best part of an hour to clean the surface. They used spatulas of soft wood at first, not scraping but easing away the seventy-year crust. Finally they washed it with cloths, taking turns up the ladder.

The stone filled the embrasure at the bottom of the narrow opening. A fraction of an inch was inset under the ashlar of the jambs of the lancet. The marks on the surface where the grime was more deeply embedded stood out sharply as Peter finished the scrub. He lowered the pail on a cord and came down the ladder carefully.

"We haven't had lunch yet!" His voice was oddly surprised. "Let's eat a sandwich while it dries."

Mig grinned at him. "Did you know it was twenty past four?"

"Didn't," said Peter wearily. "Doesn't matter. I'm hungry now!"

When they had eaten, Mig went off to wheedle materials out of Miss Pringle for making the rubbing. Their own store was at home. Suddenly it had become totally important that they should have it before nightfall.

Peter lay on his back between the tombstones of the outer graveyard.

Clinton regarded him speculatively. "Does it help us?"

"Of course!"

"How?"

"Confirmation. We could have been wrong about our crosses, but the big one up there matches ours and the other two are identical . . ."

"And there actually *is* a church where it marks one?"

"Oh, yes!" Peter was completely confident. "Rumboldswyke —here, and Appledram—or Apuldram, they spell it sometimes—here, and the position's just right for the arm of the harbor above Dell Quay and the roads are right. The Romans built them. Stane Street comes in just clear of the town. The Saxons carried on with them later—after all, they were there. And there *was* some sort of a Roman site down at the Bill. The Prof was telling us about it the other day. They found a hoard of gold coins there years ago—three hundred of 'em. Still pick up odd coins on the beach. There must have been a road down to it from the South Gate."

"It figures." Clinton considered the evidence carefully. "And there aren't any other churches?"

"What d'you mean?"

"The map covers a lot of ground," said Clinton obliquely. "Two cathedrals and only four churches? Must be more than that. Why doesn't it show them?"

Peter sat up and stared at him. "Hadn't thought of it," he admitted candidly. "It's right for our part of the map—there are only two, St. Wilfred's and St. Thomas à Becket, but there's a whole bunch between them and Chichester."

"Sure is! I've been looking at the Ordnance map."

"Why aren't they marked?" Peter's voice was thoughtful.

"Could it make a difference?"

"Dunno." Peter was worried. "I just don't know. We'll have to ask Old Mr. Ramidge."

They were still silent when Mig came back, carrying the rubbing paper. "She's going to require an hour of your valuable time in exchange."

"What for?"

"Shifting birds' nests in the rafters of the chantry," replied Mig, heartlessly. "I offered—after she'd fixed on you, of course. She said it was no job for a lady." She looked down at her dress, stained with water and pigeon. "She's right too."

"Damn!" Peter grunted. "When? She always picks awkward times. What did you say?"

"I said"—his sister looked at him sweetly—"that you'd be delighted, delighted. Wouldn't have got the paper otherwise."

"What do we do?" Clinton disregarded the interchange.

"I measured it." Peter was quite clear as to what had to be done. "Twenty-four inches by twenty-seven inside the strips of the border. We'll cut the paper roughly to that and I'll trim it up there so that it fits exactly. Be easier to keep it in place that way. We'll need weights—four of them at least."

Mig produced two pieces of lead. "Do for a start?"

Mig spread the Ordnance Survey map on the kitchen table again. They put the new rubbing overlapping the eastern side of it with the tracing of their own half that Mig had prudently made and kept.

Peter said: "At least we can see if it's hopelessly out by comparing the distance between the points we know about."

"How?" demanded Clinton.

Peter put his finger on the larger cross. "We all agree that this is Chichester. Right! We think this is Appledram. If it is, this must be the top of the harbor. We think this is Rumboldswyke. Right! We measure these up on the map and we measure them up on the rubbing. If the proportions work out about the same, then we know just about how accurate the map on the rubbing is."

"We don't know the scale of the map on the stone!"

"Yes, we do," said Peter patiently. "It's about four miles from Old Fishbourne to here." He ran his finger past the church at Rumboldswyke to the edge of the rubbing. "Must be, if you take a line down to Pagham. It's twenty-four inches on the stone, so the scale's near as anything to six inches to the mile. We can start with that."

Chapter SEVEN

"HOW did you arrive at this?" Old Mr. Ramidge's voice seemed stronger than it had been.

Peter looked at him with suspicion. "We took the angles between each of the churches that we knew and the Selsey cross and we drew them in on the Ordnance Survey map."

Old Mr. Ramidge nodded very slowly. He whispered: "They were not, of course, accurate."

"No, sir." Peter was careful. "We knew they wouldn't be. We checked that when we drew in the angles between the churches that are still there and found out how inaccurate they were, but it was the best that we could do."

"And then?"

"And then we measured the distances according to the stone map and we marked them in." He pointed to a confusion of intersecting lines and dots in the sea to the southwest of Selsey Bill.

"And you discovered?"

"That five of the lines passed through a circle with a diameter of a quarter of a mile and three of the dots were inside it."

"And you concluded?" Old Mr. Ramidge looked at him, his eyes suddenly alive.

Peter hesitated and finally plunged. "That if anything *is* left of the old cathedral, it is most likely to be inside that circle, sir."

Mr. Ramidge was silent for a long time.

Mig, watching the great panorama of the Island and the channels, dared not turn round. Clinton kept his hands tightly thrust into his pockets. Peter alone watched the old man's face anxiously.

When Old Mr. Ramidge spoke it was like an oracle making its answer. "This was intelligent. You were right to take the angles as a guide rather than the distances. This graving would not have been made by a mapmaker. It would have been made by a draftsman on the staff of the cathedral, a man who was accustomed to working with angles."

"But how did they do it, sir?"

"It could have been done by simple triangulation." Mr. Ramidge's voice was almost human. "It could have been done by using the sun at noon, or even by the Pole Star at night. They may reasonably have had a lodestone."

"But how would that—?"

"By rubbing an iron needle and floating it on a cork in a bowl of water. It would, of course, have been very early for that, but it is not impossible. Architects' draftsmen would have known of these things."

"And the distances?"

"They would have paced them," answered Old Mr. Ramidge firmly. "That is no problem."

"Is there any way"—Clinton took a hand in the conversation—"is there any way that we could have made corrections in the angles?"

"No way. I have examined them all. There is no error common to them."

"Did you work out a position for yourself, sir?"

"I did. The center of your circle should be seven hundred and seventy yards from the present end of the main road."

"We made it a little more than that," said Peter candidly. "But if we may use the point you calculated, sir?"

Mr. Ramidge said: "Use your own, boy, and have confidence in it."

"Split the difference," suggested Clinton, grinning.

Old Mr. Ramidge turned his head slowly and looked at him. "Split the difference," he agreed, and almost smiled.

Mig came from the window. "Did you work all night?"

"I need little sleep," said the old man, smiling at her. "I sit here late on many nights."

"The lights must be beautiful." Mig nodded confidently. "And there are the nightingales." The same curious understanding that had showed itself at their first meeting passed between them.

The old man said: "There are nightingales and nightjars too, and a wakened thrush, and sometimes curlews calling."

"And all the lights—right out to the Nab Tower."

"And past it to the ships going down Channel. One of these nights you must come after dark, if your mother will permit it."

"Thank you," said Mig with a complete sincerity.

They had almost reached the door of the room when Clinton turned suddenly. "Sir, why are there only four churches?"

Without moving, Mr. Ramidge said: "That is an intelligent question. There are only four churches because there *were* only four churches."

Peter saw the point at once. "You mean there were only four churches at the time that the map was made?"

"Exactly."

"And that could give a rough date for it, then?"

"Exactly." Mr. Ramidge's voice was farther away than ever and clearly final.

They went out and shut the door behind them.

Clinton almost crashed into Young Mr. Ramidge as they scurried in through St. Richard's porch.

"What happened this time?" the Master-Builder demanded.

Mig said airily: "We love your father." And with more than a hint of complacency added: "He agrees with us."

Young Mr. Ramidge was incredulous. "What about? He hasn't agreed with anybody for fifty years. I don't see how the three of you do it. Did he give you tea?"

"It was ready, but we couldn't wait." Mig was bubbling over. "Will you tell Mrs. Miles how sorry we are. Please! We just had time to catch the bus."

Peter broke in: "And we must see the Prof! Has he arrived yet?"

"He's in the Library. I haven't seen your rubbing yet."

"Could you come with us? We've got it here to show him. We've worked it all out."

They were moving across the nave.

Mig went on: "He'd worked it out too."

"And he agreed with you?" The Master-Builder shook his head. "Beats me," he said.

The Professor was standing bent at a table studying a document. He looked up as they came in. "What on earth are you three up to now? 'Lo, Clint!"

"Glad to see you again, sir."

The Professor nodded amiably. "What's this about a rubbing?"

Peter held the tube firmly in his hands. Without replying to the question, he asked: "Is there a list of the consecrations of the churches around Chichester?"

Professor Carrick looked faintly aggrieved.

Young Mr. Ramidge took over the answer. "There ought to be a list somewhere, but I think I could probably give you a rough dating."

"Good!" Peter's voice was full of confidence. "Appledram and Rumboldswyke?"

"Rumboldswyke probably started Saxon—it's mostly eleventh century. Appledram could have started Saxon too, there's early work at the east end."

"St. Thomas à Becket and Church Norton?"

"St. Thomas is eleventh century. Church Norton could be any date from about 900. It was rebuilt in the twelfth century anyway."

"And what comes after them?"

"D'you mean with the parish churches?"

Peter nodded.

"It's a fair list." Young Mr. Ramidge made an effort. "Donnington, Mundham, Sidlesham, Merston if it's in your area, Old Fishbourne—they're all thirteenth century. Most of the parish churches round here are thirteenth. There was a wave of building . . ."

"All right"—the Professor glared at Peter—"explain! Beginning with what you are pleased to call *your* 'area.' "

"It's the area covered by a map we've found." Peter was aware that the time had come to be frank. "At least we found half of it, Old Mr. Ramidge found the other half seventy years ago. It shows the Roman roads, the coastline, the cathedral, and four parish churches—all the churches are eleventh century or earlier, and—" He paused.

"And what? Don't try to hold *me* to ransom, young man!"

Peter laughed out loud. "I wouldn't dare! It's that we've only just found out ourselves. If we're right, the map must have been made before they built any of the thirteenth-century churches."

There was a long silence while the Professor and Ramidge stared at each other. It was the Professor who spoke first. He said flatly: "Can't be." He shook his head and altered his approach. "Are you thinking what I'm thinking, Ramidge?"

"I am."

"The Matthew Paris map in the British Museum is"—he hesitated for a moment—"1250 or thereabouts. What's the date of the Hereford map?"

"Twelve hundred and eighty, as I remember," said Mr. Ramidge.

"And the Gough map?"

"A lot later."

"Then . . . ?"

"It would be the earliest map in England?"

"Just precisely that. It would have to be." The Professor permitted himself a long low whistle. "Show me!" he ordered bluntly.

Peter uncapped the tube. Carefully and slowly he extracted the two rubbings; Old Mr. Ramidge had yielded up their original. Mig, almost speechless with excitement, helped him to spread them. Clinton watched, his eyes flickering backward and forward.

Peter swept his finger across the top half of the rubbings. "The Roman roads," he said, not bothering to emphasize it, "the cathedral at the cross, Appledram and the head of the harbor, and Rumboldswyke . . ."

Professor Carrick stared, fascinated. "It could be," he said after a hard-breathing silence. "It could be."

"The Roman road going down to Selsey." Peter's finger led downward. "Pagham Harbor, St. Thomas à Becket at Pagham, and the old church at Norton."

"It seems impossible—but it *could* be," said the Professor again. His tone had a newer, more definite note. "But why? What was it for?"

As if she had been waiting for the cue, Mig flattened out the last curl of the rubbing and pointed to the second of the big crosses. She said softly: "Selsey Cathedral."

"No!" Professor Carrick shook his head. "Too much! It's got to be a hoax."

The Master-Builder stroked his chin, fingers on one side, thumb on the other.

The Professor looked at him sharply. "Well, hasn't it?"

"It would have to be a very ancient hoax." The words were curiously mild.

"What d'you mean—very ancient?"

"Just about the same age as if it were genuine."

Young Mr. Ramidge caught Mig's eye and nodded comfortingly to her.

"Why?" The Professor was blunt.

"Because the bottom half of the stone—their discovery"—he looked across at Peter—"is in the foundation of the second bay of the retrochoir. It could have been inserted later, but that seems highly improbable. The top half is in the lancet in the gable of the chapel of St. Mary Magdalene—and that hasn't been restored, so it must go back at least to the rebuilding after the fire in 1187. It's plainly re-used stone, so it must have existed before the fire—at the very least."

"And they're both still *in situ*? They can be properly examined . . . ?"

Peter straightened himself with a hint of indignation.

"Shut up!" ordered the Professor abruptly. "No one's accusing you of fouling up evidence. What I want to know is if the workmen have disturbed anything. Both stones will have to be examined in detail of course—every possible test—"

"They will be." Young Mr. Ramidge's voice was suddenly terse.

Professor Carrick disregarded him, even if he had noticed the change of tone. His mind was ranging into the future.

"You three have a genius for . . ." He allowed his voice to die away. "Question is: How do we make it public? The newspapers . . . ?" Again he let his voice die away.

"Perhaps we should leave that to the Dean—"

Mig interrupted Young Mr. Ramidge. She said calmly: "We want you to keep it a secret for ten days."

"If the Dean wants it published at once . . . ? It could be enormously valuable from the point of view of the Restoration Fund, you know. He's worried about that. So are we all."

"Only ten days." Mig's voice was pleading.

The Professor came out of his private thoughts. "Why?" he barked.

"Because," replied Peter firmly, "we want to try to find it."

"Find what?"

"The cathedral at Selsey."

"You've found what may be the oldest map in England. Do you realize how important that is? I don't think you do. It's—it's stupendous! And you want to go dashing off after . . ." The Professor checked himself suddenly as if he had only just taken the meaning. "The Cathedral under the Sea? You don't mean . . . ? You can't be serious?"

"We are," said Mig calmly. "You see we know where it is—now."

"How?" Once again the Professor barked—there was no other word for it.

Hurriedly Peter spread out the Ordnance Survey map. "We took the angles from the crosses on the stone map to the Selsey Cross," he began. Carefully, surprisingly clearly, he detailed their methods, stage by stage. "We made the center of the circle about eight hundred and ten yards from the end of the main road."

"Ingenious!" The Professor's voice had lost its rasp. "Astonishingly ingenious. And you worked it out by yourselves?"

"Yes, sir. Old Mr. Ramidge worked it out last night—independently."

The Master-Builder nodded. "So that's why he was scratching about at four o'clock in the morning!"

"And?" The Professor's voice was almost polite.

Peter turned to him. "He made the center of his circle forty yards closer inshore."

"How long have you known this?"

"Since yesterday," Peter answered. "At least we've only been sure of it since yesterday. We've been guessing at it since Mig spotted the grooves on our piece of the stone."

"That was why you sent for Clinton?"

"Yes, sir. He's had a lot of practice at skin diving. We haven't."

"Have you plotted this on the chart?"

"Of course, sir!"

"What depth of water did you get?"

"Just over two fathom at low water of spring tides."

"And you think you can do it?" This time the Professor addressed himself directly to Clinton.

"Sure of it, Professor."

Peter took it up. "My uncle's boat will be ready tomorrow. It's been having a refit. We've got the rubber dinghy. Our suits are ready. We want two days to get in some practice with Clint in the harbor, and we want to talk to the lobstermen— Old Mr. Ramidge told us to—and then we can start. We could cover the circle easily in eight days, and the spring tides are in the middle of the eight days. It couldn't be better for us— if the weather holds."

The Professor looked at Young Mr. Ramidge. "The ball's in your court really. I've just remembered—this isn't Roman."

Young Mr. Ramidge said: "Not at all."

Mig allowed herself to giggle, remembering the Professor's earlier tone. The Professor glared at her.

Young Mr. Ramidge said: "I still think the Dean . . ."

"He'd *have* to say, 'Make a news story out of it.' " Peter was recalling things that his father had said. "He couldn't help himself. And we'd have every motorboat and every fool in a dinghy from Lymington to Bognor milling up and down the moment we tried to dive. *Please,* Mr. Ramidge!"

Mig looked him full in the eyes. "Your father—" she began.

Hurriedly Mr. Ramidge said: "That's hitting below the belt!"

"Meaning?" asked the Professor.

"We think," said Mig promptly, "that Old Mr. Ramidge would bring pressure to bear." She brought out the phrase triumphantly.

"That's blackmail!" exclaimed the Professor.

Mig shook her head and said primly again: "No, it's not. It's *force majeure*—we were taught all about it last term." She relaxed and grinned cheerfully at Young Mr. Ramidge. "He's afraid of his father," she explained.

"The Dean . . ." Young Mr. Ramidge made one last effort.

"The Dean's afraid of your father too. Everybody's afraid of your father except"—suddenly she smiled enchantingly—"except us."

Chapter EIGHT

THE quay was empty when they went into the locker room of the Sea School. The morning dock loungers had not yet arrived. The day was quite silent, not a breath of wind over the harbor. The water was a pale turquoise that here and there reflected colors on the shore; it had none of the deep, crisp blues that wind would give it. It was going to be extraordinarily hot. The ancient structure that had been by turns warehouse and fishermen's shed glowed in the heat with its red brick and its red roof tiles, and even the black tarred weather-boarding was hot-looking.

Mig said: "It'll be wonderful to be on the water again. I don't think the Prof's spotted that we're getting away from the digging."

"He will!" Clinton shook his head. He had a deep respect for the Professor's acumen. "Give me a hand with this!"

They shifted the air cylinders from the locker room and carried them outside. Peter was putting down his own scuba suit. Mig went back for hers. They spread everything in the sunlight, and Clinton began to go over each piece with the air of a hound on the scent.

Two small boys drifted up and stood silent.

Mig, coming through the locker-room door, groaned and said: "Oh, not Amelia! I thought we'd be too early for Amelia."

"Who's Amelia?"

"Amelia, the almost human," said Mig acidly. "Not a soul mate."

"Speak for yourself," grunted Peter, polishing the glass of his goggles.

"All right! If you'd like her to come with us—"

"Hell, no!" Peter almost exploded in his haste. "Not that!"

The sound of a sniff came over the still air across the quay meadow.

"Her cold is worse," said Mig heartlessly. "It almost always is. She can't ask us to take her swimming, anyway."

"She can and she will!" Peter retorted. "D'you think we could take her out one of these days and mislay her?"

"I'm sure her mother wouldn't mind." Mig's tone was unfeeling.

"Sharp," said Clinton, looking up at last. "Sharp and tidy. I like the nylon lining. I'm glad you went for wet suits. 'Tisn't as if you were going diving off Spitzbergen. When you've finished picking the neighborhood folk to pieces let's have a look at the face mask." He peered at it, said "Okay!" and, stretching out his hand, picked up an air cylinder. "Certificate all right?"

"Six months ago," Peter replied. "It's just been refilled."

"My brother's got a new one, better than that," said a voice that Clinton identified at once as Amelia's.

"Has he?" Clinton answered automatically, as if he had been forced to do so.

Mig snorted in the distance, examining the straps of her flippers.

"Yes, he has—and he's got a better diving suit too! Where are you going?"

Clinton found himself identifying the sneakers and the bare legs and finally the brief shorts that belonged to the voice.

Again he answered compulsively: "Middle of the channel, outside the Isle of Wight."

"You're not," said the child calmly, and sniffed. "Are you
diving for treasure?"

"Doubloons," replied Clinton foolishly. "Pieces of nine."

"Eight," the child corrected him, and sniffed again.

"You haven't allowed for inflation."

"What's inflation?"

Clinton looked desperately at Mig for help. Mig studiously
avoided his eye.

"It's when the pound goes down and the mark rises and the
dollar drops." Clinton took a fraction of a second to wonder
why he was doing this.

The sniff coincided with the second. "I don't believe you,"
said Amelia calmly. "You're American, aren't you?"

"Want me to sing 'The Star Spangled Banner' to prove it?"

"Yes," Amelia answered.

"I ought to've known better. Help!" Clinton groaned.

"You started it," said Peter unsympathetically. "You finish
it."

"I didn't start anything. *She* started it. G'way! Go and sit on
the grass and commune with nature or something."

"I like it here. When are you going to start diving for
treasure?"

"I never said anything about diving for treasure."

"You did! You said doubloons in the middle of the channel."

One of the small boys asked: "Are you reely goin' to dive
for treasure?"

An old man, one of the regular dock loungers, came past
and his shadow fell across the suit. He said amiably: "Blow
your nose, Amelia!" and sought out his accustomed place.

Clinton finished his inspection of Mig's suit and began on
Peter's. There was nothing defective in either of them. He

opened the duffle bag that contained his own and began to go over it with the same care. Amelia kept up a flow of comment and question; it never ceased except when she was forced to blow her nose. Clinton secured a momentary silence only when he told her that she ought to have her adenoids out and she announced, after considering the matter for a moment or two, that she would have to tell her mother. It was, he realized, a generalized threat.

Another old man came down the quay, and behind him a thin man wearing a gray suit and an expensive hat.

Amelia, after studying the stranger for a little, decided to transfer her attentions. "They're going to dive for treasure," she announced.

"Are they?" answered the thin man rashly.

"Yes, they are. For doubloons in the channel."

The man's voice was lazy, clearly he was just indulging a child, but something in it caught Mig's ear as he asked: "What channel?"

"Bosham Channel," replied Amelia, having failed to take in Clinton's extravagant misinformation.

"They are, are they?" said the man, and using the exchange as an introduction, added: "That's a pretty fair suit you've got there."

Clinton said shortly: "It's Italian."

"And you're American?" The voice had a rising inflection.

"Sure."

"Water's a bit muddy for skin diving in the harbor."

"Sure," Clinton repeated.

"Going outside?"

Clinton glanced across at Peter, who was frowning. "Just going to try out the suits," he said reluctantly. "Doesn't much matter where."

"Good luck!" said the man kindly and moved off to the end of the pier.

The first of the old men asked: "You the two that's stayin' in Major Manson's place?"

Peter said: "He's my uncle."

"See him in the bar of the Anchor, times. He's right about the mud." He nodded over at the man in the gray suit. "You go on down to Bosham Deep—plenty o' water there."

"We might do just that," said Peter evenly.

"What boat you usin'?"

"My uncle's."

"Aah! The *Snail*—Tom Callan told me he was bringin' 'er round if there was still water enough to float 'er when he finished the job."

"When'll that be?" asked Clinton.

The old man studied the mud with an experienced eye. "Half an hour he'll have still, mebbe."

"Why *Snail*?" asked Clinton.

"My uncle doesn't like speedboats. She's not exactly fast but she gets there."

"What you going to do till then?" demanded Amelia.

"I could think of half a dozen things I'd like to do," replied Clinton sharply, staring at her.

Amelia backed away three paces. She said carefully: "I don't think I like you."

"That makes two of us!"

The *Snail* came up in a generous curve and slipped into the narrow deepwater channel between the piles and the quayside.

Peter caught the stern line and made it fast to a bollard. He took the painter and made that fast in turn. Then he squatted down on the edge of the quay and said: "Thanks, Mr. Callan. We didn't think you'd make it before the water went."

"Did though—just," said Mr. Callan. "Want to see the ladder?"

Peter lowered himself down to the solid, sturdily built boat.

Tom Callan took him aft, and they leant over the counter. "Two rungs under the water," he said. "Couldn't have more. Would a' had to bolt it too close to the rudder. Put it farther out, the outside corner'd hit something every time she went up the beach an' lay over. Trick's to get your hand on the top rung an' jerk yourself up so's you can get your foot on the bottom one. You'll come out all right."

"Much better than trying to pull oneself over the side." Peter nodded. "Safer too, I reckon. It was my uncle's idea."

"Goin' to try her out?"

Peter wriggled silently. There were too many questions. He had thought they could slip away quietly. Some of the questions he couldn't budge. He answered slowly: "We thought of going down to Bosham Deep."

"No fish in Bosham Deep," said a new small boy, sitting precariously on the string piece.

"No spear gun." Clinton came to Peter's aid.

"No treasure either." Amelia had stolen up on them again.

Peter had a sudden and genuine inspiration. He looked up to the quay and said: "There is too!"

"What?"

"The Great Bell of Bosham."

The two old men nearby guffawed in unison. One of the small boys laughed, the other two looked doubtful. Amelia was plainly baffled.

Peter climbed up again. "Let's change!"

They slipped inside the locker room before the laughter died. Mig was in her suit already: she met them as she came out.

Clinton gave a wolf whistle and said: "Getting a big girl now."

"Clinton Hammond!" exclaimed Mig furiously. "You'll get your face slapped."

"Sure," agreed Clinton gleefully. "Sure!"

Peter was slower, a little awkward, less used to diving gear than Clinton, but he finished at last. They put on their watches—Clinton's was an elaborate panel of watch, compass and depth gauge—checked with each other's instruments, and went out.

Amelia said scornfully: "They haven't got their flippers on."

Mig was already in the boat. The boys joined her, stowed their gear and squared away the loose oddments on the bottom boards. There was just enough water to get the *Snail* away from the quay. They were familiar with her from earlier runs with their uncle; details had been changed since the last time they'd used her, but nothing that mattered.

Peter pressed the self-starter and the motor came to life. He looked up at the line of legs and foreshortened bodies that stood like a palisade along the edge of the quay above them. "Somebody cast off the bow line?" he called.

The eldest of the three boys, hovering patiently above the bollard, stooped and dropped the line inboard.

"Stern line!" It was freed and tossed amidships.

Peter put the engine astern and they gathered way, slowly edging down through the muddy shallows to the open water. When he was certain that they were clear of the slipway, he put the engine ahead, and they came round in a wide curve and headed into the anchorage. Gulls rose, squawking.

Peter wiped his forehead. "Phew! I couldn't have taken another question."

"It's Amelia," said Mig darkly. "I think she's a child witch."

"It's everybody!"

"What's this Great Bell of Bosham thing?" demanded Clinton.

"Nut story," Peter answered. "Lot of 'em round the English countryside. Like the men of Zennor."

"What about them?" Clinton was plainly confused.

"They got talking, in the local pub or somewhere, about summer and how it was only summer when the cuckoo was there, so they went out and built a wall round the cuckoo."

Clinton laughed dutifully. "And?"

"Listen to him!" Peter turned to his sister.

"I think—I just *think*—he's putting you on." Mig frowned at the American boy.

"It was worth trying," said Clinton modestly. "He rose all right. I still don't see what it's got to do with the Great Bell."

"The Danes raided this place." Peter swept his hand round in a circular gesture. "They burned Bosham—they burned the palace and they burned the church. They stole the Great Bell and loaded it into a long-ship, and they took off. They had two men of Bosham prisoners. The prisoners prayed, and the local saint—no, come to think of it, it couldn't have been a saint, Bosham church is Holy Trinity—anyway, somebody—took a hand and the bottom of the ship split open and the Bell sank into the Bosham Deep."

"And?"

"One of the men made a mark on the gunwale of the ship to show where the bell went down—so that they could find it later."

This time the laugh was genuine.

The anchorage was way behind them now, the forest of masts growing smaller and smaller against the harbor trees and the distant and beautiful line of the Downs. A pair of swans flew low across their bows, but the motor was making too much noise for the three to hear the harp song of their wings. A brace of mallard inshore against the Cobnor side took off with enormous purpose and settled as purposefully a hundred yards beyond. High above them, so high that they were only dabs of white against the blue of the sky, a score of gulls were soaring in slow, easy spirals on the ascending thermals.

Mig, lying back against a cork cushion, said comfortably: "It's lovely to be living."

"How far's this Bosham Deep place?" asked Clinton.

" 'Nother quarter of a mile."

"How deep's Deep?"

"Bit over two fathom, same as the patch we'll be working in."

"That's good. What's the tide?"

"The rise? Sixteen foot eight off the Bill; I looked it up this morning. That's the top of spring tides. Be about three foot less than that in here."

"And it's about the beginning of the last quarter of the ebb now?"

"Little more than that."

"So"—Clinton made a quick calculation—"we ought to have sixteen feet under us if we've made our quarter of a mile."

Peter bent down and switched off the engine. The heavy boat carried her way against the tide for a little and finally stopped. He said: "Let go!" and Mig dropped the lighter of the two anchors over the bows.

Clinton adjusted the straps of the harness, fastened his weight belt, put his bottom on the gunwale amidships, and swung round until his feet were in the water. "Okay, Mig!"

The girl went through her own drill, testing valves, making certain that straps were tight, and finally settling her face mask comfortably. They were not wearing hoods.

Peter crossed over to the other side of the boat, balancing. He noted that it made little difference.

Clinton let himself down neatly into the water, fixed his own mask and waited. Mig copied him carefully. Clinton put in the mouthpiece of his aqualung, raised his hand in a signal, and, as he saw Mig fit her own mouthpiece, slapped her on the shoulder and let go. The tide swept them down the side of the boat. He noted the speed of it automatically and did a surface dive. Mig followed him. They went down together. The water was thick and murky, but they could see each other well enough in the first feet. Clinton led to the bottom. It was just possible to see the surface of the deep mud, with waterlogged branches embedded here and there. He noted a tin and some-thing that might have been a saucepan. They drifted past them with the tide at a speed that was disconcerting. After a moment or two he made a signal with his thumb up, pointing at the surface. Mig put up her own thumb in answer. She pulled at the lower strap of the harness, settling it more comfortably, and struck up.

Clinton moved a little away from her, watching her closely. She swam well, using her flippers to the maximum. Her train-ing clearly had been sound; all that she wanted was practice.

The light increased rapidly and they came to the surface, level. Clinton lifted his head, spotted the boat well to the left of where he had thought she would be and perhaps fifty yards uptide, and, dipping again, began to swim back about five feet below the sunlight. Mig copied instantly and intelligently. He noted that she was looking at the compass on her wrist from time to time. He thought: she'll do.

It took them longer than he had estimated to get back to the boat. The tide was strong. He was not sorry when he got his hand to the gunwale. He hadn't swum for more than a month. Taking out his mouthpiece and pushing his face mask on to his forehead, he said: "Good girl, Mig! Anything I can do, you can do better—or just as well, anyway. Up the ladder!"

He watched her carefully. She crooked one arm through it and unconcernedly took off her right flipper, tossed it inboard and, groping down, took off the left in turn. Then she looked up at the ladder, judging the length, grasped the top rung and jerked herself as Callan had suggested. She shot up, her foot found the bottom rung and she climbed sedately on board.

Peter clapped ironically.

Clinton glared at him. "Your turn!"

They went through the same routine again. Clinton noted that Peter hesitated before letting go and that he took longer to adjust his face mask. He was, he decided, less deft than Mig, less assured, but he swam strongly under water and it was clear that he knew what he was doing. They missed the saucepan this trip but there was a new sardine tin glinting in the light, and just as they reached what Clinton judged was the point of return, they heard the sound of an outboard's propeller hurtling toward them. They watched a skiff pass overhead, flashing light at them and making magnificent patterns of bubbles in the sun of the surface. Clinton let it get safely away before he gave the signal to go up. Oddly, he was tired this time when they got back to the boat.

Peter tried out the ladder, flippers and all, and decided when he finally scrambled into the boat that it was a mistake. Clinton had already thrown his inboard.

They settled themselves comfortably in the hot sun, using the lifesaving cushions.

Peter asked finally: "Okay?"

"All okay," Clinton replied. "You may even live."

Mig giggled.

"Only thing's the water. You're certain it's clearer offshore?"

"Certain," said Peter. "It has to be."

Mig asked: "When do I go in again?"

"When your instructor says." Clinton grinned at her. "We've got all morning and the sun's hot." He lay there lazily, thinking things out.

Chapter NINE

MRS. MANSON gave them the envelope when they arrived for lunch—late, as usual. She was entirely calm about the lateness; she always was in the holidays. There was a covering note inside the big envelope from Young Mr. Ramidge and a second envelope, addressed to John Eartham, Coxswain, the Selsey lifeboat. The letter said: "Father insists that you see Mr. Eartham. The note will introduce you. Father's about ten years younger this morning and he says you're intelligent. I *think* this covers all three." It was signed with Young Mr. Ramidge's initials.

"The Prof brought it," said Mrs. Manson. "He's going to Bristol this afternoon, but he said no matter what plans you had, you were to see Mr. Eartham today. I asked him why." She took an enormous pie out of the oven, clanged the door, and added abstractedly: "He said because Old Mr. Ramidge said so. Everybody's frightened of him."

"Except us," repeated Mig dreamily. "Did he say a time?"

"No, but you'd better get there reasonably early. The Kellogs are coming tonight."

Mig put her head on one side. "It's hot and it's enormous. If we've got to eat it, we'll miss the three o'clock bus."

"Not if you hurry."

"If we hurry"—Peter considered the matter very carefully —"we'll get indigestion."

"You mean you're trying to talk me into driving you to Chichester bus station."

"Never crossed their minds," said Clinton sardonically.

"If you've got the car out—" Mig began again.

"And you're on the by-pass—" Peter took up the attack with expert gamesmanship—"it isn't really much farther down to Selsey."

"Nine miles!" His mother allowed a little acid to creep into her voice.

Together the two of them said: "Eight miles from the by-pass, and you love driving!"

"Like a comedy duo," said Clinton scornfully. "Why d'you fall for it, Mrs. Manson?"

Mrs. Manson only laughed.

Mr. Eartham regarded them with an extremely clear but mildly frosty eye. "What would it be about?"

Peter held out the envelope. "It's a note for you from Mr. Ramidge."

"The one at the cathedral?"

"*Old* Mr. Ramidge," put in Mig rapidly. She was beginning to have a very clear idea of the value of the name.

"O-o-ld Mr. Ramidge"—the coxswain stretched out the first vowel—"a-a-h!" He took the letter, opened it carefully and read for a moment. Looking up under bushy eyebrows, he said: "And you would be Peter Manson?"

Peter nodded.

"And your sister and"—he consulted the note again—"and Clinton Hammond."

Mr. Eartham returned to the note. For a little he read in silence, having trouble with the minute, spidery hand. ". . . under the water," he said at last. "Where else would it be? And he reckons *you* can find it?" He looked up from the note

again and stared at each of them in turn. "He must think"—
it was disconcerting listening to his frankness—"an awful lot
of the three of you. There's hundreds tried it. Hundreds!"

Peter attempted a last throw. "We think we know roughly
where it is," he said, slowly and carefully. "And Old Mr.
Ramidge thinks so too."

"A-a-h!" breathed Mr. Eartham, and it was apparent that he
had accepted them. "Then you'd better tell me all about it,
hadn't you? Come along inside. Mrs. Horsley, d'you think we
could have a cup of tea? Four cups o' tea? And you were
bakin'?" He lowered his voice again. "Sit!" He waved his
hand round the small neat room. "Now!" he said questioningly
as they settled. "Where do we start?"

"We've found a map." Peter spread both hands wide in a
gesture that was half surrender. Carefully and slowly he out-
lined the discovery of the two halves of the stone and the
method by which they had plotted the position. When it was
done, he paused, watching the coxswain's face. It was utterly
expressionless. Peter decided to fire his final shot. "Old Mr.
Ramidge worked it out too. There was about forty yards difference between us."

"And?"

"We split the difference." Mig smiled at him.

"You did what? You got Old Mr. Ramidge to . . . ?" He
raised the note again and read for a moment. "You did too!"
he said abruptly.

Mrs. Horsley came in with a tray. Mr. Eartham climbed to
his feet and walked over to the wall. The Admiralty chart of
the area was spread across it. When Mrs. Horsley had disappeared, he raised a finger and stubbed it on a point south of
the Bill. "Sand," he said, "mostly sand with rock underneath.
Scours off sometimes when the wind's with the tide. Loose
boulders, gravel. All sorts."

"We guessed—we hoped it would be protected a bit by The Grounds and The Dries."

The coxswain looked round at Peter sharply. "You can't reckon . . ." he said severely.

"We know." Peter nodded hastily. "What we don't know is the tides. We need help badly there."

There was no apparent response to the plea, but finally Mr. Eartham said: "The last lot, they had a bit of bother at times —the Sub Aqua Club lot from London—but they were a long ways out, t'other side of the Mixon. Tide comes pretty sharp through the Looe Channel. Three tides meet there. It's tricky. Ebb runs two and a half knots. You won't get that much inshore, not where you're thinking about. Knot and a half at springs—wouldn't be more, might be less." He seemed to be talking more to himself than to the three of them. Presently he said, ruminatively: "Slap in the middle o' the two-fathom patch. How would you reckon to go about it?"

Hesitantly Peter produced a folded sheet of paper from his pocket. Without opening it, he said, "We'd like to lay a marker on the exact position."

"How?"

"We think we could get a fix by using the windmill, the Mixon and the Coastguard tower."

"Fair enough. And then?"

"We'd put down a small buoy." Peter made a gesture with his fingers shaped and curved to indicate a sphere about the size of a football. "Dinghy mooring with a socket. We'd put a flag in it when we were working. We've planned"—he opened up the folded sheet—"we've planned a square search. Do the inshore half first, lay another marker about two hundred and twenty yards uptide of the center buoy, and anchor the boat downtide two hundred and twenty yards below it."

"Why there?"

"We reckoned it'd be the best place in case of an accident.

We've got my uncle's boat and a rubber dinghy with an outboard."

Mr. Eartham wheeled on them suspiciously. "And the three of you'd work from the dinghy?"

Peter shook his head. "Two at a time. The third would stay on watch in the boat in case anything went wrong. We think the best thing to do is start at the uptide end of the square, one man swimming down while the other handles the dinghy. Then both men go back and the second man swims *his* leg. After that the first man changes with the boat keeper. We reckon we'll get the most rest that way."

Mr. Eartham said: "Sound common sense. What d'you reckon to see?"

"We hoped we could manage a strip ten yards either side of the swimmer if the water is clear. We're looking for something that'll be pretty big—part of a wall perhaps—at any rate big squared stones."

Mr. Eartham took a long time to consider this. Finally he said: "Wouldn't build too much on seeing a full ten yards either side. You'd need to be lucky with the water. You'll need to be patient too." Something in the words "you'll need" implied consent, even cooperation.

Mig sensed it before Peter did. She asked: "You think we can do it, then?"

"Didn't say nothing about that," replied Mr. Eartham cautiously, "but you've got good ideas—some o' them. You'll need luck with the weather too." It was clear that he left nothing to chance. "How long d'you reckon it'll take you?"

Peter considered the point with care. "We talked Young Mr. Ramidge and Professor Carrick into giving us ten days. We've got nine left. If we take three days over the inshore half—and we think we could do the shallows pretty quickly with snorkel—that'd give us six days for the deep water."

" 'Slong as you don't get ideas about rushing it."

Peter shook his head. "We've got ten days before they tell the newspapers about the map—they've promised us that much —and we've promised not to say anything about it ourselves before that."

"Old Mr. Ramidge," said the coxswain with emphasis, "told me I wasn't to give you away."

"We were a bit worried about the lobstermen," began Peter.

"You leave their pots alone, they'll leave you alone," said Mr. Eartham briskly. "Fred Harling, he uses that bit o' water most. I'll have a word with him."

"It's very kind of you," said Peter politely.

"You thank Old Mr. Ramidge! Seen the coastguard yet?"

"Your letter only came at lunch-time," Peter explained, "and we were late for lunch."

"Got another for Jim Perrin?"

Mig shook her head.

"Then that's what he means when he says"—Mr. Eartham referred to the letter again—" 'and *anybody* else able to be of assistance to them.' I might ha' known!" Mr. Eartham allowed himself to chuckle for the first time. "I'd better take you along to Jim Perrin myself. He's a friend of mine."

"*Not*," said Clinton critically, "the Queen of the South Coast watering places."

"For an American you know too much about England . . ." began Mig, and went on helplessly: "It *is* pretty awful, isn't it?" She turned away from the sea and looked down the un-made track littered with parked cars that crowned the untidy line of the sea wall until it collapsed in great slabs of broken concrete. The high tide sucked in and out of the unlovely breakwaters. "It's better at low water, when you can see the beach."

"It'll need to be!" said Clinton acidly.

Peter asked: "See what I meant about the way the end of the road looks as if it's been cut off with a knife?"

Clinton stared at the unconvincing railing that marked the end of the roadway. It required no effort of imagination at all to see an older road heading far out over the sea. The entire coastline, despite the elaborate system of wall and small breakwaters, had a raw and impermanent air, as if it were part of a colossal engineering project and the bulldozers had only lately passed that way.

A flurry of small boys hurtled by them and went down the steps to the water. They began to throw pebbles out to sea.

"What do they do the rest of the time?" demanded Clinton.

"Wait for the tide to go out." Mig grinned down at the smallest of the small boys, and then waved her hand up the coast toward Portsmouth. "Bracklesham Bay—that's where people find coins—but nobody knows where the Roman settlement was. There was a Saxon village halfway up to East Wittering."

Peter leant against the rails, peering to the southeast. "The Sub Aqua people believe that they've found a Roman fort beyond the Mixon."

"Is that the Mixon beacon there?" Clinton pointed.

"That's it. They reckon they found catapult shot and the walls of a fort."

"Was it?"

"I don't know that they've proved anything," replied Peter cautiously.

"And we work . . . ?"

Peter searched the water for a moment. "D'you see two buoys out there—close together? That's the entrance to the Looe Channel. Dark one's the Street, t'other one's the Pullar. They're about a mile and a half out—almost in line with the end of the road here."

A car turning short round at the end of the roadway almost backed into them. Its driver hooted indignantly after the manner of motorists.

Clinton said indulgently, as it went off in a flurry of exhaust smoke: "Isn't anywhere else for 'em to go. When they're here, they're here. How far does the tide go out?"

"Long way at dead low water, springs."

"Then low tide, we'll be all among the bathers?"

Peter grunted. "Can't be helped. We'll get that part done as early as we can."

Clinton said: "I thought Mig might have liked it."

Mig snorted.

Clinton ignored her. "Pretty public," he said thoughtfully.

"We can't have 'em warned off," Peter protested. "It's a free country!"

"And by the second day somebody's going to ask what we're doing!"

"The coxswain of the lifeboat knows, the coastguards know." Mig summed up rapidly. "Nobody cares about holidaymakers —they forget things anyway."

"And we *have* to be straight off the road end?"

"That's where the lines cross," Mig reminded him.

"And one line runs from the end o' the road?"

"No," Peter answered. "We didn't use that for fixing the position. We aren't certain that this was the line of the Roman road. The old main road of the village went off to the south-west, to where the coastguard station is, but there's a map in the cathedral that shows a track from it in a straight line to here. We think it could have been the ancient road."

Chapter TEN

"TRY it again," said Peter contentedly. "I think we've just about got it." He brought the *Snail* round in a wide, easy curve. "We'll have to make a bit more allowance for the tide. I'll tell you when I've got her lined up with the road. Clint, you know what to look for now. Shout just before you get the top of the sails of the windmill in line with the coastguard flagstaff. Mig, you let go the anchor as he shouts. Got it?"

He straightened up the boat and the rubber dinghy came into protesting line astern of her. Gulls hanging over the still, blue sea watched them hopefully. There was only the faintest breath of wind and that blew lazily from the eastward. They could hear the shouting of the bathers on the beach. Peter lined the *Snail* up carefully with her bow precisely notched on the end of the road a little over half a mile away. He had throttled right down, and she moved silently. He made small corrections from time to time, allowing for the tide. He felt under his skin a tingle of excitement.

For three minutes they held the new course. Then Clinton muttered warningly: "Coming up!"

Peter kept his eye on the end of the road and the line of the buildings on either side.

Clinton watched his marks and barked: "Stand by!"

The boat went on. A gull swooped suddenly. The dinghy yawed off a little to starboard. Clinton's voice snapped: "Mark!"

Mig jerked at the stock of the anchor balanced over the bows, and, as it splashed into the water, Peter put the gear lever into the astern position, checked the boat's way and switched off. All three sat quite still, listening to the galvanized cable of the anchor chain running through the fair-lead. The noise ceased, began again as the cable pulled out a few more links, and stopped once more.

Peter said: "Give it two or three fathoms, Mig, and we'll start checking up. If we're where we ought to be, the Mixon should bear about a hundred and twenty-three degrees and the Looe Channel buoys should be in line dead astern of us."

"They are," said Clinton cheerfully, and reached for the hand-bearing compass.

The boat began to swing to the ebb tide. Peter craned his neck over the starboard quarter and peered down through its shadow. "Bottom's clear—not perfect but clear enough. I can see flat rock bottom and two big stones. Rest is sand." He listened to the chain running out for a moment longer and then said: "Make that fast!"

Clinton said: "Hundred and twenty-two degrees."

"The Mixon?"

"What d'you think? The girl in the blue bikini?"

Mig said: "You shouldn't have known there *was* a girl in a blue bikini!" And they all laughed suddenly with relief.

Peter put the chart board on the top of the engine casing. "Come on! Let's get four separate bearings and see where they put us. I think we're just about right."

They argued happily one by one over each fresh sight but in the end even Peter was satisfied. It seemed unlikely that they were more than twenty or thirty yards at the most from the position that they had plotted with such pains for the cross on the stone map.

"Can do," said Peter at last. "I don't think shifting her all over the landscape will help us. All we need is to be somewhere in the center of the circle. This *is*."

The *Snail* rode easily with her bows to the tide, the light easterly air was nowhere near enough to swing her. Peter studied the gurgle of water past the rudder and the little trail of bubbles that ran out from it.

Behind him Mig asked: "Next?"

"Let's put down the mark buoy." Peter moved into the midships compartment and freed the coil of nylon line that had been placed there carefully before they set off. He examined the heavy galvanized iron grapnel that they had discovered in his uncle's tool shed, checked the splice, and turned his attention to the little red mooring float. When he was satisfied, he steadied himself, swung the grapnel experimentally, said: "Here goes!" and flung it well out to port. As the line ran, he picked up the float and tossed it over. It bobbed serenely, drifted a little astern of them, and settled in its place, the tide sucking at it as it passed.

"I think we got the depth about right. It'll still have something in hand at high tide. Let's lay the uptide marker."

The problem of fixing the limits of the square that they proposed to search had bothered them. Clinton had produced the solution. From the clutter of old fishing lines in the Major's toolshed they had made up a length of two hundred and twenty yards, marking it at twenty-yard intervals with colored cloth. Mig made it fast now to the bows of the *Snail* and handed the coil to Clinton, who had hauled the rubber dinghy alongside and was holding it in position. Peter started the outboard motor, and with Clinton paying out the measuring line, the two boys took the dinghy away up the tide, keeping the *Snail* precisely astern. The colored rags slipped out with astonishing speed; at a hundred and eighty yards Peter slowed the motor until he had barely steerageway. They came

to the last marker rag with the dinghy creeping forward, and
Peter said: "Drop!"

Clinton tossed over a heavy lead weight with a thin nylon
line attached. A little day-glow flag, with its bamboo shaft
stuck through a big cork float, was made fast at the end of it.

Peter had shut the engine off altogether now, and they
drifted back to the *Snail,* hauling in the measuring line and
coiling it down in the bottom of the dinghy. When they were
close to the boat again, he turned round and said, pleased:
"Shows up all right. We didn't need a bigger flag." Of Mig,
watching them from the bows of the *Snail,* he asked: "D'you
think we were right for the line of the tide?"

She waved her left hand lazily. "Bit over to port, but I
didn't think it was enough to shout about."

Peter reached with a boathook and at the second attempt
got hold of the mark buoy. Fixing its larger day-glow flag in
the socket and making it fast, he put the end of the measuring
line through the ring in the bottom.

"Let's take the *Snail* down to the base line and see how it
looks!"

Clinton joined him in the bows. They worked well together
without need for explanations. Now they hauled the heavy
boat against the tide, tripped the anchor and began to raise it
as she dropped away from the bobbing mark buoy. They let
the tide move her, watching the colored rags go overboard
and trying to judge speed. As Mr. Eartham had told them, it
would be less than a knot. This time they re-anchored the boat
at the end of the measuring line. Looking uptide, the central
marker buoy was absolutely clear. The small flag beyond it was
a little more difficult to see when the breeze blew the little
patch of silk away from them; even so it was plain enough.

Peter looked at his diving watch. "With a bit of luck we can
make three dives—one each." He looked across at Mig. "Clint

and I'll try it first to see how it goes. You're boat keeper!"

Mig nodded. It was the sensible arrangement. "If I'd brought my dark glasses, I could sunbathe." She looked at her brother out of the corner of her eye.

"You could *not!*" Peter almost shouted. "You'll watch us and watch us carefully. If anything goes wrong, you start the motor, cut the lashing of the anchor cable, let it run, put her in gear and come over to us—and you don't waste time!"

Mig smiled angelically and irritatingly. She answered, and her voice had an entirely spurious meekness: "Yes, brother."

The boys slipped on the top halves of their diving suits, put the aqualungs into the dinghy, put their face masks over the tops of their heads, and dropped in their flippers. Mig could see Peter going item by item over his equipment in his mind, his mouth moving as he shaped the names. She knew that he was worried—worried because he was completely conscientious.

Clinton was nonchalant about the whole thing, but even he rechecked before he lowered himself carefully into the dinghy.

As Peter started up the outboard, Mig leant over him and touched his shoulder with the back of her knuckles. "Luck!" she said, and he looked up at her and relaxed a little, and grinned.

The dinghy chugged away, straight up the line of the tide toward the center mark. In a little it hid the mark buoy. They freed the measuring line and headed up for the small flag. There was a brief delay there, and Mig went aft, found the binoculars and moved up to her place in the bows again. Focusing the glasses, she watched Clinton slinging off his harness; he was going to make the first dive then—that was sensible too. She watched as Peter slowed the dinghy close to the small mark flag and saw Clinton slide over the side and disappear. The outboard motor clearly was throttled back until it was just ticking over. With the distance and the soft east wind she could hear nothing except the noises along the beach and car horns, and once, far away, the nervous upcurving shriek of a frigate's siren off the Nab. Very slowly the dinghy drifted down. Sometimes it moved broadside on to her; once it turned completely and she could see the outboard motor; once it went off, clearly under power, to the left and turned and came back again. For the most part, however, it just grew slowly larger and larger. It passed the center mark clear of the red float and came on—two hundred yards away now.

Peter was silent, staring absorbedly over the side of the dinghy. He was between Clinton and the sun, using the shadow of the dinghy to watch him. She knew that he had nothing to tell her or he would have shouted, and she forbore to ask questions. She could see bubbles on the water now when the fitful east wind left the surface untouched. Clinton had passed inshore of the center mark, Peter to seaward, and they came steadily down the line, closer and closer. Finally Peter seemed to become aware of Mig. He straightened himself, looked over at her, and lifted up one hand with his thumb high in the air. Mig returned the gesture. The bubbles were getting very close. She began to stare through the water too.

When she saw Clinton, he was swimming easily, moving in little zigzags to either side. She guessed that he must be keeping direction by the sun over his right shoulder or by the dinghy or both. He moved smoothly, entirely unconcerned, and, as she watched, he curved up suddenly just beyond the boat anchor and, the great flippers moving rhythmically, propelled himself toward the boat. Even then she was not ready for it when his hands shot out of the water and grasped the gunwale and she felt the *Snail* give to his weight.

Peter brought the dinghy in on the other side. "Smooth— everything worked! He came down like a dream."

Clinton, on the other side of the *Snail,* pushed up his face mask—the mouthpiece of the aqualung was already out—and grinned at her. "One saucepan, half a plate, two tins, and a lot of rocks."

Mig smiled back at him. "We didn't expect anything on the first run, did we?"

"Nope, but it would have been kinda nice." He hauled himself round the stern of the *Snail* and up the other side to the dinghy and slithered aboard it.

Peter said: "Want a spell? How was it?"

"No spell. We want to see how long it takes to do three runs. Get an idea of the size of the job that way. It was easy. The water runs just fast enough if you zigzag a bit."

"How much d'you reckon you could see?"

"With the zigzags, ten yards either side, like we hoped."

"Nothing that looked like anything?" Peter's voice was almost wistful.

"Nope," repeated Clinton firmly, and undid his weight belt. He slipped off his harness and his mask and put them carefully out of the way. "Let's go!"

They waved to Mig and moved off, Peter revving up the outboard this time in a cloud of spray. She wondered how they would measure twenty yards from the little mark flag, and assumed that they would guess it. Once more she picked up the binoculars. Peter was settling the aqualung over his shoulders. She saw him adjust the mouthpiece and, as she watched, saw Clinton turn the dinghy sharply and bring it past the uptide mark, heading in toward the shore. It lost way, and she watched Peter turn and slide over the rubber of the dinghy's side. Then, in turn, he disappeared.

Peter had not used the glass-bottomed box, but she saw Clinton try it a few times. Finally he stowed it away. It seemed to her that Peter was moving slowly. Above him, Clinton made wider zigzags; once or twice he seemed to back up slowly against the tide, as if he had seen something that he wanted to examine more closely. They came past the center point a good twenty yards inshore, and she began to check her own equipment. It was all there. She was aware of the growing excitement. This was the first time that she had ever dived in the open sea. Clinton had made it look easy, but things like this came easily to Clinton. She wondered how Peter had taken it and she knew that her heart was beating faster and faster.

Clinton started calling to her cheerfully from forty yards away: "Him like porpoise man. Heap big swimmer."

She waved back, oddly comforted. Finally, Clinton turned the dinghy diagonally toward the boat. He passed the bows, circled and came up on the port side. This was evidently agreed procedure, and as she turned she saw Peter coming up from the bottom. He moved confidently—not as smoothly as Clinton had done but well enough. She knew now that it was going to be all right if she could manage as well herself.

Peter came up toward the stern of the *Snail,* worked his way round to the ladder, threw in his flippers and climbed aboard. "It was great! That's the longest I've done yet. It went like a bird."

"Fish," amended Clinton.

"All right, fish then."

Dryly Mig demanded: "But did you see anything?"

Peter looked crestfallen. "No. Rock and sand and boulders."

Clinton said: "This isn't a moon shot de-briefing. Say what you have to say and let the Queen of the South Coast aquanauts make her run! We're doing this against the clock. D'you want to spoil our statistics?"

Mig laughed and felt better. She passed her gear over to Clinton and followed it.

Peter said: "Take it easy!" and she made a face at him. He

took a towel and dried his hair, watching the rubber dinghy diminish.

The whole scene looked different from the rubber dinghy. It was lower in the water to begin with, and it was noisy and the water tended to slap against it. But it was lively and fun. Mig laughed suddenly, and Clinton looked at her and grinned.

The center mark flashed by them, and he shouted above the engine noise: "Kit up! You're going over in two minutes."

There was excitement in everything: in securing the harness straps, in adjusting the weight belt, even in pulling on the face mask. She wasn't aware of the outside world now; she had forgotten about the beach; forgotten about the ketch that she had watched, working its way through the Looe Channel against the tide; forgotten about the frigate that was swinging for compasses off the Nab. Her world was narrowing down to the face mask and the aqualung and the little circuit of the undersea that would be its limits. She was fleetingly aware of the flag of the uptide marker. She felt the dinghy lose speed and the outboard go silent. Then she felt Clinton slap her bottom and shout: "Over you go!" and she slid over the side of the dinghy as they had practiced it in Chichester Harbor, and automatically made a surface dive. She went down to a patch of sand fringed with rounded boulders and squinted up over her right shoulder to find the position of the sun. Then she began to swim.

For three minutes she milled, concentrating on her stroke and on her searching. Clinton had said, "Zigzag," but she was a little uncertain still. Finally she remembered to look for the dinghy, and because she could not find it instantly, had a sudden fleeting moment of panic. Then she saw it, silhouetted and extraordinarily clear, just ahead of the sun, its propeller turning idly and every now and then breaking a little flood of bubbles. She began to zigzag.

It was quite silent down here except that she could hear very occasionally the whisper of the propeller. Silent, still, and astonishingly clean, the rocks were sharply edged, the sand was white. She saw no half plates, not even a tobacco tin. It was a world of green. Even the white sand had a green tinge, and only the rocks were dark and foreign in this serene composition of aquamarine light.

Chapter ELEVEN

MIG unzipped the top half of the suit and hung it over a thwart. She let herself down limply on the bottom boards amidships and groaned: "I'm pooped!"

Peter shrugged his shoulders. "So are we all."

From his own private snug Clinton declared: "Not me. I'm fresh as a li'l daisy."

Peter disregarded him. "Six dives and not a sign . . ."

He lifted up the lucite-covered board which protected their diagram. "We've done a strip a hundred and thirty yards wide by a quarter of a mile, and not a single thing—not one single, solitary thing except tin cans, a rusty anchor, part of an iron bedstead—and what that was doing there beats me!—a gas cylinder, and an awful lot of rock."

Clinton, with his sun hat tipped over his eyes, intoned: " 'We don't expect to find anything with the first dive. We know we've got to work for it. We—' "

"We don't like being reminded of what we say to grownups," said Mig acidly. "We feel that it is better to keep a decent veil over some things. We don't think much of this patch of water but we consider it will be better farther out."

"We *hope*! All the same, it'll be dead low water in thirty minutes and we planned to do the shallows come dead low water."

"First we paddle, then we wade, then we use snorkel."

"Clever girl! She remembers what she's told."

Mig was too tired even to make a face at him.

Peter ignored them both. Casting his mind back to the list of things seen, he said: "We forgot the lobsters. I saw seven altogether. How many did you see?"

"Six," said Mig.

And Clinton said: "Six, me too."

"We'd better tell Fred Harling. I still wonder why somebody dropped a new gas cylinder there."

"Was it new?"

"Looked new enough."

"Busted valve," suggested Clinton. "You get mad at 'em. Which end do we start workin' the shallows?"

" 'Bout the middle, I should think. We'll take a look with the dinghy. The low-tide mark cuts across the corner of our square, I think."

Clinton said: "If the two of us work together, we can cover the shallows fast."

Mig murmured sleepily: " 'One man in the boat, one man in the dinghy, one man in the water.' "

"Not in the shallows!" protested Peter.

"You don't mind the local hell-children mucking about with the dinghy when you're snorkeling?"

"I hadn't thought of that!"

"They stick knives into rubber dinghies to see if there's really air inside."

Peter surveyed the crowded beach and wrinkled his nose. "I thought they'd have gone back to lunch by now."

"Not this lot," said his sister. "They take their lunch in installments all day. Do we know exactly where the corner of our square is?"

"We've got to fix it. The little marker that we dropped when you started the last dive is a hundred and ten yards from the center line—halfway. Corner of the square's another hundred and ten yards in. Looks from here as if the low-water mark's about halfway in between and going across diagonally to the southeast."

"You *could* make it even more complicated if you tried," murmured his sister, with an edge in her voice.

The water was almost absurdly still. The noise of a group of five small boys running through the shallows toward them seemed ridiculously loud. Behind it the only background was the burr of voices on the beach and the rasp of a transistor radio punctuated with occasional car horns.

The dinghy drifted in with just a whisper under the wet rubber of her bows. The leading small boy called: "Pull her up for you?" and looked puzzled when Peter said: "Leave her! You can help shove me off in a second." To Mig he said: "Out you go! Start paddling!"

The small boys pushed the dinghy off, watched Peter start the motor, and splashed on after Mig. Their leader asked: "Lost something? Can we help you look for it?"

Mig hadn't bargained for this. She invented shamelessly. "We're making a chart for ourselves. We don't like the one the Admiralty made."

"What's a chart?" demanded the biggest of the boys.

Mig decided at once that they were vacationers; local boys would have known all about charts. She tried a little embroidery. "There are different kinds. We're making a conger chart. We're conger hunters."

"Congers?"

"Congers is eels," said the smallest boy.

"That's right." Mig nodded approvingly. "Big eels—they live in wrecks."

"Do they bite?"

"Always!"

The smallest boy considered the possibilities of danger. "Hard?"

"Very."

"My mum said not to go into deep water."

"Your mum's right. I've got to go in deep."

"Can you swim?"

"Like a conger," said Mig outrageously. "Can you?"

"No," replied the smallest boy, crestfallen. "I better go back to my mum."

"You wouldn't want her to worry about you," Mig agreed with him tactfully.

The whole group decided to go inshore again. They splashed off through the shallows on a herd impulse. Mig plodded on through the water.

The serious bathers were in a congested area more or less off the end of the road and between that and the point of the Bill. She would have to go straight through it—but bathers never really noticed anything. She began to concentrate on the search. Oddly enough, it was more difficult than it had seemed farther out. The water was not as clear inshore as she had expected it to be and the light reflected off it curiously so that it was opaque at short distances. It hardly mattered though; none of them expected anything as close in as this. It was just that Peter was conscientious—the diagram had to be filled in— the area had to be marked "searched"; he had a tidy mind.

She plowed on doggedly. There were outlying bathers now, but nobody took any notice. She avoided the worst of the splashers, passed through the bathing area, and gradually reached into deeper water. She was more than waist-deep when she came level with the line of the *Snail,* floating peacefully a quarter of a mile out to sea. She could make out Clinton watching, and waved, and he waved a lazy arm in return.

Following the plan that they had agreed, she moved twenty

yards out—the water was almost up to her shoulders now—and moved back parallel with the shore again. There was nothing on the bottom. Here and there a ridge of gravel, a few large pebble areas, one isolated boulder—nothing more. Peter came in with the dinghy as she finished this second leg. He had been moving slowly up and down all the time that she was wading.

"Nothing," he said gloomily. "Not a damn thing! You?"

Mig opened her hands palm outward. "Nowt!"

"Any bothers?"

"No bothers."

"Right! Take her up to the marker." Peter pointed out the tiny, almost invisible flag. "Grab it, cut the motor at the same time, and steer out to sea. Drop it again when she stops and just let her drift till you're level with the *Snail*. Nothing to it. Use the shadow for looking and the glass-bottomed box if you're doubtful."

He pushed her out, watched her critically as she started up the motor, and struck off to do his stint of wading. A few minutes later he heard Clinton start the motor of the *Snail*. The tide had turned in the deep water. He looked for the dinghy and saw Mig wave to Clinton. She knew what she had to do when the tide turned inshore. He splashed on determinedly.

When Mig came inshore at the end of Peter's second leg, they didn't even bother to exchange the inevitable "Nothing." As he got ready to push the dinghy off, she stopped him. "I'm baked. Ices all round?"

He nodded. "Two each. It's hot. You've earned it. Got any money?"

"I always remember the important things," said Mig loftily. She splashed ashore and walked diagonally toward the steps at the end of the road.

The smallest boy intercepted her, faintly apprehensive. "Find any congers?"

"Not a cong," said Mig.

The small boy appeared relieved, and drifted off.

She picked her way through deck chairs and sand castles and rows of bathers and climbed the steps. A row of people leaning over the rail inspected her as she came up. She stalked a little self-consciously past them to the beach shop, bought six cups of assorted flavors, and walked back. Only one person was leaning over the rail now, a man. He seemed vaguely familiar.

As she reached the head of the concrete steps, he said: "I know you. Met you on Bosham Quay. You were going skin diving."

Mig felt a prickle of irritation. She remembered him—the thin man in the gray suit—the nosy one. It wasn't exactly what she would have called a "meeting."

He was still nosy. He asked: "Lost an anchor or something?"

Mig answered shortly: "No."

Unabashed, the man said: "You seem to be searching up and down. That's your boat out there, isn't it?"

Mig nodded, there didn't seem any point in denying it. They would have to go straight out to the *Snail* anyway. "My uncle's," she said abruptly, and began to go down.

"Fine weather for seeing things under water," said the man, ignoring her tone. "Hope you find what you're looking for."

Mig's "Thank you" could have been put more curtly, but not much. When she was clear of the nearer sunbathers she half-turned and looked back. The thin man had gone from the rail. A moment later she saw him among the parked cars along the unmade road. When she looked a second time, he was gone.

As they headed off toward the *Snail,* Mig said above the noise of the motor, her face close to Peter's ear: "I met Nosy ashore."

"Nosy who? One of those kids?"

"All kids are nosy. No, Nosy in the gray suit in Bosham."

"What was he doing?"

"Watching us," answered Mig calmly.

"How d'you know?"

"He told me."

"Don't believe it! Why should he?"

Mig made a face at her brother. "He asked, 'Lost an anchor or something?' "

Peter looked at her, mildly bothered.

"And after that he said, 'You seem to be searching up and down.' "

"Did he, by Christmas!"

"And he finished up, 'Hope you find what you're looking for.' "

"Heck!" snorted Peter, and throttled back the outboard. He followed Mig back on board the *Snail* and said: "Tell him!"

"Ices!" Clinton regarded them thirstily.

"No, oaf! We've been spotted." Quietly Mig recapitulated the conversation.

"Did he seem friendly?"

"Too friendly." Mig's voice was tart.

"D'you think he has anything to do with the cathedral? Chichester cathedral, I mean."

"Never seen him there." Peter's voice was full of doubt. "I think we know just about everybody on the staff."

"Ancient Monuments people? Or whatever they're called?"

This time Mig shook her head. "They'd know about us and the Prof. He'd have said something."

"And what happened then?"

"He disappeared among the parked cars."

Clinton scratched his ear. "Probably sitting comfortably in one now, watching us."

"Probably."

"What do we do?"

"Nothing. What *can* we do?"

"We can see if we can spot him with the telescope," suggested Peter.

There were people sitting after the fashion of motorists in seven of the twelve cars that they could see, but the telescope gave them very little aid. It was by accident that Mig spotted with her naked eye the man with the gray suit on the beach. He was walking casually on the dry sand between the families and the castles. Peter had the telescope. Mig pointed him out and Peter focused the glass and watched him for a moment.

"Can't place him," he said and passed the telescope to Clinton.

Clinton adjusted it and settled himself more comfortably. The others talked across him, getting nowhere. After perhaps two minutes he said: "Hell! My ice is melting: You can—wait a minute!"

"What?"

"Talking to somebody—kids! Small boys. Three of them!"

Mig almost snatched the glass from him. It took her a moment to find the thin man. When she found him, she said instantly: "The kids who helped us when we went in the first time."

"Did you talk to them?"

"Yes—they were nosy too."

"Did you tell them anything?"

"Of course I did!" Mig looked scornfully at him for a moment and put her eye back to the telescope. "I told them we were conger hunters."

Clinton laughed delightedly. "He can make what he likes out of that!"

There was a little pause. "He will," said Peter thoughtfully.

"He'll know that there aren't any congers here unless he's half-baked and he'll know we're covering up something."

"What else ought I to have done?" asked Mig defensively. "They were only kids. I didn't know he was there then!"

"Nothing," said Peter. "It can't be helped."

"But at least we know that he's watching us. Anybody at Bosham we can ask about him?"

"We can try."

Chapter TWELVE

CLINTON was steering. He demanded: "See it yet?"

Mig shook her head. "Not a sign."

"You looking in the right place?"

"Of course I'm looking in the right place!" snapped Mig indignantly.

Peter put down his notebook. He had been entering up times and distances. "You ought to be able to see it by now."

"All right, you come and look!"

Peter swiveled round on to his knees, looked over the bows to starboard and said: "There it is!"

"Well, it oughtn't to be there," said Mig defensively. Both the boys laughed. "All right, gang up on me!" She had picked up the red float now. "It's a lot farther out than it ought to be."

"*You* think!" Clinton grinned infuriatingly at her.

Mig glanced inshore rapidly. "We're level with the coast-guard station. The Mixon isn't where it ought to be."

"Moved overnight," said Clinton derisively.

Mig snapped back: "The buoy's moved!"

As Clinton began a rejoinder, Peter said: "No, wait! I think she's got something. We'll have to take the bearings again."

Mig said triumphantly: "*And* it's going to be farther to the east than it ought to be."

Peter acknowledged uneasily: "You may be right."

They came down to the buoy and turned to seaward of it,

stemming the ebb. It was about half tide.

"Looks all right," said Clinton.

"It is," said Peter, "but the bearings are all wrong. Look at the Looe Channel buoys!"

"Look at the end of the road," said Mig. "We're way out of line."

Clinton revved up the engine until they were level with and just inshore of the buoy. Then he said: "Drop the hook and let's take the bearings all over again."

Mig let go the anchor.

Once again they went painstakingly over the bearings, made a new plot on the chart, and regarded the results suspiciously. Peter measured it up with plodding accuracy. "Three hundred yards south-southeast of where it ought to be. Must have dragged." His voice was rueful.

"Why should it?" demanded Clinton. "There wasn't any wind in the night."

"Not wind," said Peter crestfallen. "It's high water of spring tides today. We couldn't have allowed enough line."

"Meaning?" asked Mig.

"That the buoy floated the grapnel off the ground and it came down here with the tide."

"Don't believe it!" Clinton shook his head. "It's a heavy grapnel. We put it down pretty near high tide. There was plenty of line to spare."

"All the same it shifted," persisted Peter.

"Next thing"—Clinton disregarded him—"if it did float off, it would be on the rising tide. It should have finished somewhere that way." He stretched his arm out in the direction of their route from Chichester Bar.

"It could have floated back."

"On the way the tide ran yesterday, it wouldn't have gone south-southeast, even if it had, which it wouldn't have."

"Elegant," put in Mig. "But I see what you mean. I think you're right."

"What then?" Peter's forehead wrinkled.

"Somebody"—Clinton's voice was exaggeratedly casual—"shifted the damn thing."

"Who?"

"Lobster boat?" Clinton's voice rose a little.

"Why would a lobster boat be moving south-southeast from where we dropped it?" asked Mig.

"Going out to another set of pots," suggested Peter reasonably.

"But there weren't any pots inshore of us when we left last night and there aren't any now." Mig ran her eyes over the inshore water.

"A yacht?" asked Clinton.

"We left pretty late. Wasn't a sign of anybody about then, but there could have been later of course. All the same, anybody with any sense would've been farther out with the evening coming on."

"Dinghy then—catching the line on his centerboard."

"Could be, but it was too late for dinghies."

"Well, who would want to shift it and why would they just shift it three hundred yards or so? It doesn't make sense. It must have been an accident!"

"All right then," Clinton nodded agreement. "It was an accident. What do we do now?"

"Pick it up and put it back in the right place," said Peter determinedly.

"Not till I've had a look at it," said Clinton. "At the grapnel, I mean. Don't suppose it will tell us anything but we ought to look." He began to zip up his suit.

Peter pulled out the glass-bottomed box and went into the bows. Lying well over, he placed the bottom of it in the water and hunched down to look through it. They heard his voice muffled and resonant from inside the box: "Grapnel's out of sight. Sand bottom, and a bit of rock—over to port. Looks about four fathoms, could be a bit more."

"Okay." Clinton slipped on the harness, tested the straps, felt his weight belt, and pulled down his face mask. He lowered himself over the counter of the *Snail,* turned with his feet in the water and, avoiding the dinghy, slipped away from the boat and submerged.

They watched him as he swam strongly uptide, getting deeper and deeper as he followed the line of the mooring of the buoy. Peter went back to the glass-bottomed box and, with it, followed him a little longer. Clinton disappeared. There was nothing more to see except the bubbles. They waited.

Twice Mig looked at her watch. He seemed to be gone an awfully long time. Twice she looked questioningly at Peter.

He growled at her finally and said: "He knows what he's doing."

"It just seemed . . ." Mig did not bother to finish the sentence.

After a long pause, she tried again. "D'you think he'll find anything?"

"Depends whether there's anything to find," said Peter hesitantly.

The bubbles had moved over to the left, well away from the point where they knew the grapnel must lie. Now they went uptide in a wide, shallow curve. Clinton was carrying out an oddly elaborate search. The bubbles moved inshore of the *Snail* and stayed for a long time almost stationary.

Peter began to fidget then, and he was still fidgeting when two hands appeared suddenly above the gunwale of the *Snail* and Clinton's head shot up into view. He moved up his face mask, coughed to clear his throat, and eased himself down to the ladder. As he slipped off his harness, he said, marshaling his thought carefully: "If it dragged with the tide, the grapnel would score a mark in the sand. Agreed?"

"Should do," said Peter.

"If it was dragged by a power boat, it would plow a furrow. Agreed?"

"Agreed," said Peter.

"If it floated just touching the bottom, it would scrape a little mark before it dug in and held. Agreed?"

Peter nodded this time.

"All right. There's nice clean sand all round it. No seaweed, no pebbles, no muck." Clinton paused for a moment and added: "No marks."

"Meaning?" Mig was genuinely worried now.

"Meaning that it was dropped here on purpose. Can't think of any other way. When we made marks on the bottom the first day, they stayed. There ought to be marks, and there aren't." He dried his head on the towel, put a finger in his ear and rattled it.

"Then somebody wanted us farther out."

"Why?" demanded Peter.

"Dunno." Clinton flicked up the towel.

"Who?" asked Mig.

"Search me." Clinton flicked up the towel again.

"What ought we to do?" Mig was plainly worried.

Peter said determinedly: "Go back to the old position. We said we'd search it and we've got to do that."

"D'you think we ought to tell Mr. Harling?" Mig was still worried.

"Tell him what?" asked Peter. "That the buoy shifted three hundred yards in the night? What would he say?"

"Pretty damn careless," said Clinton lazily.

"That's about it," acknowledged Peter resignedly.

Mig looked at him sideways. "I still think that we ought to tell the coastguards."

"Nothing to tell them." Peter went over the point again. "Just that the buoy shifted. I vote we go back and start all over again at the old position."

The other two were silent.

"Take a vote," said Peter. "What about you, Mig?"

"I suppose so," said the girl reluctantly.

"You, Clint?"

"Not me," answered Clinton coolly. "I'm staying."

"You're what?"

"Staying around for a bit." Clinton elaborated his decision. "There's a little old tombstone down there that I want to take a look at."

"A little old . . . a tombstone . . ." Mig and Peter brought out the words simultaneously. "You don't mean—you can't . . ."

Clinton looked at them wickedly. "Likely it isn't a tombstone. I don't know about these things. It was kind of standing up." He held up his note board. "Like this." There was a crude drawing on it that showed a rough slab just projecting from the sand. It was more or less rectangular, reaching up in a triangle.

Mig said: "You're unspeakable, Clint! You sat there not telling us, arguing . . ."

"Are you sure?" Peter ignored the complaints. "D'you think it was cut stone?"

"Dunno," replied Clinton quietly. "I think it could be, that's all. It's over there." He half-turned and pointed to the water where the bubbles had remained for so long. "There's no rock near it, only sand and a couple of boulders. It's different. They're rounded, it's squared. It isn't a building block—at least, I wouldn't think so."

"How big is it?"

Clinton stretched out his fingers. "Top edge is about three and a half of these. Can't tell with the others, they go down into the sand—but deep."

"Any carving on it?"

Clinton shook his head. "Weed, I think. Some kind of barnacles, you can't tell. Shellfish anyway. Do we stay?"

"We stay." For once Peter's voice was almost as terse as Clinton's.

Mig, not even bothering to declare that she had changed her mind, said: "They'll think we haven't noticed that the position is different. That could be a good thing." Her voice had an upward turn as if she asked a question.

Peter answered it as such. "It could be, you know. If we stay and work from here, they'll think we're . . ." He paused for a moment.

Clinton said: "Suckers."

"And that might be useful," said Mig hastily. "They know who we are. We don't know who they are—except for gray suit, that is. It won't hurt if they think that we're stupid."

"They could be right at that," said Clinton airily. "Who's coming down with me?"

Chapter THIRTEEN

THEY took the agreed drawing in to Mrs. Manson. They had argued it, they had criticized each other's efforts, they had visualized again the long minutes in which they hovered in the green translucence of the bottom light, moving round the stone to judge it from every angle. They had remembered the feel of it to their fingers, remembered its surface as they chipped the dead and ancient shellfish with their knives from its edges. The drawing remained singularly unconvincing.

Mrs. Manson inspected it carefully. She hesitated perhaps a fraction of a second too long.

Mig said: "Not impressed?"

Hastily Mrs. Manson said: "I don't know. The top—if this is the top—looks straight enough but the sides aren't really at right angles, are they?"

Peter said: "That's one of the things that's important about it."

Mrs. Manson nodded. "It does sound possible but you'll need to know more about it. Could you clear the sand to show a bit more of it?"

Clinton said: "We scooped a little way here"—he put his finger on the drawing—"and then I ran my knife down. You could feel the stone and it went in the same line."

Mrs. Manson took refuge in ignorance. "I don't know about these things. What do you want to do now?"

Peter looked at the other two and said: "Scout around first and see if there's anything else. We don't know anything about this area yet except just round where we anchored."

Mig said casually: "The mark buoy shifted a bit and we were checking . . ."

Clinton's voice overrode hers. "I was swimming away from the grapnel when I saw it. Everything else we've seen so far was rounded or jagged." He let his own voice trail away and Peter went in to bat.

"We've been looking for straight lines all the time—squared stones—mason's work."

"Yes, I see. Well, it looks as if you've made a start anyway. It's a pity . . ."

Mig's voice was startled. "What's a pity?"

"The glass is dropping." Her mother's voice was quite genuinely sympathetic.

Peter muttered pessimistically: "The mare's tails."

The three had watched the delicate wisps of cloud forming high to the southwest as they ran up to the Chichester entrance.

"Perhaps it won't come to anything." Mig tried the effects of a little optimism.

"It always does," said Peter somberly. "Just when we've made a start. Just when the tide's right. Just when we've got time off."

"If you can't go out tomorrow," said Mrs. Manson sweetly, "you could go and see your Aunt Ethel."

Her son and daughter turned on her in a single lightning movement. "Nicer children than us have left home for less," said Mig bitterly.

The casement window tapped so gently that it was hardly more than a bird's footfall on a tin roof. Peter woke instantly as if he had been waiting subconsciously for it. The window creaked out again and this time, as the wind caught it, it banged. He climbed out of bed, sleepy and furious at the same time, fumbled with the catch and slotted it home. In the darkness behind him Clinton's voice said: "I suppose it's from the southwest?"

Peering up through the top panes, Peter could see moonlit clouds scudding up from the direction of the Isle of Wight. "Southwest, of course," he agreed gloomily. "It couldn't be anything else. What do we do now?"

"Wait and see what it's like in the morning." Clinton was flatly practical.

Peter grunted. After a long silence he asked: "D'you think we ought to have told Mother?"

The two of them knew each other's minds well enough not to need to be specific.

Clinton answered: "Mig did! I've never known anybody get away with things the way she does. I was scared stiff your mother'd ask questions when she said the buoy had shifted. Mig wasn't. She put it in just at the right moment, when your mother was thinking about something else."

"I'm still not sure," said Peter uncomfortably.

Clinton stared up at the ceiling in the faint glow of the outside moonlight and remarked casually: "I'm not sure of anything. I'm not sure why anybody would want to do a thing like shifting a mark buoy. Isn't any sense in it. Wouldn't be the lobstermen?"

"Fred Harling was happy enough when we saw him last. He wouldn't do a thing like that."

"Wouldn't be amateur anglers?"

This time Peter just muttered: "No."

"It was too far out to bother the bathers."

Peter nodded in the darkness.

"Couldn't be a rival archaeologist? You get nuts amongst archaeologists just like anywhere else."

"They'd have said something first—complained to the Dean or talked to the Master-Builder or something like that."

There was a long silence. Then Clinton made a sound that was almost a chuckle. "You don't suppose it's Old Mr. Ramidge—not himself, I mean somebody he's sent round because he wants to have the glory for himself?"

Peter was shocked. He demanded sharply: "Do you?"

"No, but it was fun to think of it," confessed Clinton amiably. "I've been turning it over and over. I've thought about most everything possible. Trouble is it mightn't be anything at all."

"But we decided it couldn't be an accident."

"I know—but it still could be. I just thought of one chance. Bit of driftwood turning over in the tide. It might have picked the grapnel off the bottom and let it go again with another turn later on."

Peter milled this one over. Finally he recalled Mig's earlier words: "Why would it come south of the line of the tide like that?"

"Dunno," said Clinton gently, and went to sleep again.

The sky was gray and the racing southwesterly clouds seemed to come in waves, flooding over the level of the land.

Mig woke the boys. She called through the open door: "It's blowing half a gale from the southwest. I couldn't sleep and I don't see why you should. What are we going to do?"

Peter sat up crossly. "I could have done with a bit more sleep."

"Not with me about," said Mig pleasantly. "Get up and help me get breakfast."

"Virtuous this morning?" snarled Clinton from under the bedclothes. "What are you after?"

"Always eager to serve."

"Always ready to try to get something out of your mother! What's it this time?"

"If we can't take the *Snail* out today, it would be nice if Mother could drive us up to see Old Mr. Ramidge. We ought to go, you know. We said we'd report progress—and this is progress."

"So?"

"So Peter takes Mother breakfast in bed—having brushed his hair for once"—she surveyed her brother dispassionately— "wouldn't do you any harm to wash, either. And Mother says, 'What can I do for my loving and intelligent children today?' and Peter says modestly, 'Take us for a little drive in the car, like up to Old Man Ramidge.' "

Peter grabbed a slipper and threw it at his sister. She dodged it with the skill of long experience.

Mrs. Manson kept them in suspense until after they had washed up the breakfast things and tidied their rooms. Then she said airily: "I've got to go up to Midhurst anyway. I shall start about ten."

"And you expect to retain our respect and affection?" asked Mig bitterly. "You might at least have told us before we did the washing up."

Her mother smiled sweetly at her.

Peter grunted: "I'll go and ring Mrs. Miles."

Mig watched him go, balefully.

Clinton tossed a pebble from hand to hand, grinning cheerfully at Mrs. Manson.

She let them off an hour later at the steep drive that led up to the house. Mrs. Miles had indicated that they would be welcome and had managed somehow to convey the impression that they would have been even more welcome if they had called to report two days earlier.

Old Mr. Ramidge was in his chair. He greeted them without any attempt to turn his head, but the rustle of the voice was plain enough. "As soon as I saw the barometer begin to go back I expected you." Then, after a slight pause: "Found nothing." It was more an assertion than a question.

"We're not sure," said Peter. "We want advice."

Old Mr. Ramidge made no attempt to answer this.

Peter asked nervously: "Can we begin at the beginning, sir?"

"It would be appropriate." The old man's voice was distant.

Peter spread the blow-up of the chart that they had made for their diagram. They had spent most of the previous evening working it out. The coastline with the sea walls was clearly marked in. The square that they had begun to search was drawn in red. The tracks of the dives were marked in blue —long, more or less straight lines with occasional zigzags where they had made wider diversions. The right-hand half of the square was almost covered. Between the low-tide paddling and the shallow-water work that they had done with the drifting dinghy there was an irregular strip not more than a few yards in width but expanding at the seaward end into an irregular triangle.

Peter said: "We've covered all the blue part, sir. Wading or with the snorkel or with the dinghy where it was shallow enough, and the aqualung farther out. There's nothing there. We've examined every patch of rock in this area. We're certain that there's no"—he hesitated for a moment—"masoned stone anywhere where we've searched." He waited while the old man bent forward to peer at the diagram.

After a long time he asked, whispering: "This was the position we plotted?"

"Yes, sir. We laid the mark buoy there."

"And you have still to search the remainder of the square?"

"Yes, sir, except—except that we dived here." He put his

pencil on a green circle that lay half on the edge of the square and half outside near its southeast corner.

"Why?" demanded Old Mr. Ramidge without any vestige of expression.

Mig answered: "The mark buoy"—there was the very slightest hesitation—"shifted. It looked wrong to me when we went down yesterday morning." She decided not to go into detail but said simply: "When we took the bearings again, it was here." She touched the green circle.

Mr. Ramidge allowed himself to nod, pursed his lips and whispered: "Why?"

Clinton took up the answer. "I went down to see if I could find out why it shifted."

Old Mr. Ramidge was silent. Only when they thought they were clear they heard the whispered voice: "And did you?"

"No, sir."

The old man appeared altogether uninterested in the reply. Instead he asked shrewdly: "And what *did* you find?"

Mig's eyes turned to him with admiration. He missed nothing, whatever his age. She decided to leave the answer to Peter.

Her brother separated the drawings from the diagram and laid them on the reading rack. "Clinton spotted this when he went down to look at the mooring. We all examined it and we're all agreed that this is about as near as we can get to what it looks like."

"And you think?"

"That it's dressed stone, sir."

"Why?"

"Just about everything else we've seen on the bottom is rounded."

"Except the rock patches," put in Clinton. "Some of the rock's pretty rugged."

Peter took it up. "The top is squared—we're sure of that,

sir—and the upper side." He indicated the sloping face of the right-hand part of the stone. "We're almost sure it's mason's work but"—he looked candidly at Mr. Ramidge—"it isn't a right angle nor is the other corner."

"That was observant," said Old Mr. Ramidge. "And it makes you think?"

"We aren't agreed," Peter confessed. "We've argued it every way we can. I think it could be a Saxon gravestone, sir; but there's nothing to prove it. Clint thought it was a tombstone at first, now he thinks it could be a gate post. Mig feels it might be a lintel or a seat slab, something like that."

Old Mr. Ramidge nodded without giving anything whatever away. He settled back in his chair a little and appeared to go to sleep.

The three waited, exchanging glances now and then. Peter was bothered, not quite sure whether they ought to stay.

Old Mr. Ramidge came back to life gently but suddenly. The thin silver voice asked: "But why did the mark buoy drift to the southeast?"

Peter's head jerked as it always did when the old man came up with his sudden surprising insights. "We don't know," he answered honestly. "There was no wind . . ."

"I was aware of that," whispered the old voice without expression. "And the tides ran, I take it, as the diving lines run."

"Yes, sir, just about."

"It could not have dragged to the southeast then without assistance?"

"That's what we think." Mig nodded. "But whose?"

Without any emphasis to his questions, the old man extracted everything from them. The man in the gray suit on Bosham Quay. The questions. His reappearance at the top of the stairs at Selsey. The fresh questions. The talk with the small boys. The absence of signs of dragging.

At the end Peter opened out his hands helplessly. "There's nothing to go on, sir. Nothing at all. It could just be that he's—"

"Nosy." Mig finished off his sentence for him. "But why?"

"And how could he have shifted the mark buoy?"

"He hasn't got a boat," Mig rushed in.

"We don't know that." Clinton scratched his ear.

"Not at Bosham anyway," Mig snapped back.

"But he could have one anywhere from Birdham to Southampton."

Old Mr. Ramidge disregarded the spat.

They were all silent suddenly, as if all were aware that he had something to say.

He let them wait for a long minute. Then he said: "Why should they put it down again over the only piece of masoned stone in the area?"

Chapter FOURTEEN

YOUNG Mr. Ramidge peered cautiously into the road, made
certain that it was clear of traffic, and turned toward Chichester. "I've no idea how you do it"—he addressed nobody
in particular—"but you've tamed him completely. He's been
civil to me for four days. Unparalleled!"

"We like him," said Mig. "It's a bit like tiptoeing in and out
of an orchestra rehearsal, but we seem to have got the hang of
it."

Peter said something vaguely about "a new interest in life."

"New interest, my foot!" said the Master-Builder explo-
sively. "You've made an old interest possible, that's all. You've
given him the chance to laugh at the lot of us at the age of
ninety-two."

"Hooray for him!" murmured Clinton placidly.

The Master-Builder grunted suspiciously.

Mig turned and glared at Clinton. "Why," she demanded,
"d'*you* think they dropped the buoy right next to the stone?"

"Accident." Clinton shrugged his shoulders. "Luck. Chance.
Coincidence."

Young Mr. Ramidge had arrived just as they were leaving,
and Mrs. Miles offered them an improvised lunch. They had
spent the best part of an hour and a quarter thrashing over
every possible aspect of the position, and had arrived nowhere. The Master-Builder was as puzzled as any of them.

He said, after a little silence: "I think he's right. You should at least tell your coastguard friend. There may be nothing at all in it but you've nothing to lose by letting him know. What was my father saying about flares?"

"He jumps ahead so," said Peter seriously. "He's always a lap in front of us. He asked if Uncle had supplied us with flares."

"And?"

"Uncle had. I think he's thought of just about everything. And your father said, 'Keep them where you can get at them quickly.' " He considered the possibilities for a moment and added: "They're for night work, though. We won't be out at night."

The Master-Builder nodded. "They'd see them from the tower at Selsey, by day too. They're pretty much on the spot, the coastguards."

"I hadn't thought of that," said Peter.

"Well, I would." Young Mr. Ramidge managed to make it an instruction without being positive. After a moment he asked: "Where do you want me to put you down?"

Mig said innocently: "Anywhere on the Selsey bus route."

Clinton, on the back seat, laughed outright.

"Meaning?" asked the Master-Builder.

"She's going to try to wheedle you into taking us all the way to Selsey," he said heartlessly. "That's the tone she uses with Mrs. Manson."

"Twerp!" Mig's voice was scathing.

Mr. Ramidge grinned. "I owe you something. I'll take you down."

Mig closed the car door and said through the half-opened window: "It's excruciatingly beastly, isn't it? We'd come straight back with you, but we must talk to people."

The Master-Builder laughed at her and slipped in the clutch.

When he had gone, they turned back to the sea. The tide was far out but a surprisingly angry surf raced in across the shallows. It was not the exquisite snow foam of a tropical beach, but a dirty brown succession of crests of broken water with a green and malevolent sea beyond. On the Mixon it was breaking heavily in clouds of spray. They could see the black ridge of the reef clearly from where they stood. The clouds were low-bellied and lead-colored, and the Isle of Wight to the westward was almost black and altogether inhospitable. Only the inevitable frigate, swinging for compasses off the Nab, seemed unperturbed by it all. Even the gulls were querulous and wind-battered.

They went down the steps on to the firm sand with the wind tugging at their clothes and hair. It was the best way to the coastguard station.

Mr. Perrin was standing outside staring at the weather, when they reached him, cold and a little battered. He said: "At least you had the sense not to come in the boat."

"Heavens, no!" gasped Mig, with an exaggerated shiver.

Peter said: "We knew by midnight what was on."

Mr. Perrin nodded approvingly. "What can I do for you?"

Peter hesitated. "I don't think it's anything," he answered doubtfully, "but Old Mr. Ramidge thought we ought to tell you."

Mr. Perrin tapped his pipe stem a little impatiently as Peter was silent again. "Tell me—what?"

"Our mark buoy shifted, night before last."

"Well?"

"We don't see how it could have." Peter's tone was uncomfortable.

"Why?"

"Because we think the mooring was heavy enough."

"What did you use?"

"Boat grapnel," replied Peter. "Heavy one."

"And one of those li'l dinghy mooring buoys?"

Peter nodded.

"Ought to've been all right. Where did it finish—up or down?"

Peter guessed that he meant in relation to the tide. He shook his head. "South-southeast, about three hundred yards *across* the tide."

"Funny," muttered the coastguard. "Now why did it do that?"

"That's what we don't know." Mig looked at him seriously.

Mr. Perrin grinned. "No harm done. You found it all right. D'you suppose you could do with a cup of tea?" He led the way indoors and made the tea himself. Over the scalding cups he asked bluntly: "Find anything yet?"

Peter considered for a moment and nodded. "One stone— one cut stone. At least we think it's been cut but we're not certain yet." He described it roughly with gestures. "We haven't told anyone else except Old Mr. Ramidge and the Master-Builder."

Mr. Perrin looked at them humorously. "I won't either," he assured them. "Let me know if it shifts again." It was clear that his mind had gone back to the mark buoy. It switched again to the stone. "Where did you find it? Where the buoy was first?"

Clinton spoke for the first time. "Slap on where the buoy was—second!"

Mr. Perrin took in a long draught of tea, paused for a moment, and said quietly: "Now that's funny too."

They could have cut back to the lifeboat station by the roads but it seemed more satisfactory to go along the beach again despite the wind; for one thing, they were warm with tea. The beach itself was utterly empty, the surf broke appreciably closer in now with the rising tide. A big ketch was lying well over to the wind beyond the Mixon. A cutter was coming in under bare poles. An Admiralty tanker, empty and riding high, was going to sea.

Clinton asked: "What did you make of him?"

"I don't know." Mig was frankly puzzled. "What did *he* mean, 'That's funny too'?"

"It is," Clinton mocked her amiably. "He probably thinks it's a lot of hogwash."

They walked in silence. Level with the concrete steps, Clinton turned away.

"Where are you going?" Peter asked.

"To take a peek in those cars," said Clinton cheerfully. "You never know."

Mig frowned. "Gray suit?"

"I'm beginning to take a kind of interest in that guy." Clinton went off, whistling.

The other two looked sidewise at the three cars that were parked on the front, their windows hermetically sealed against the wind.

Peter said once: "You never know," but otherwise they did not talk.

Under the great slabs of broken concrete on the point Clinton rejoined them. "No gray suit," he said succinctly.

The beach shelved rapidly here and the water was close in to the shore, but there was still room enough to walk below the level of the sea wall on shingle. They deserted it only when the proper path began.

As if the climb up to it marked a period in her thinking, Mig said: "I don't get it—I still don't get it!"

"Nor do we," said Peter. "Let's go and see if we can find Mr. Eartham!"

The coxswain was out "somewhere up the village." They went back to the sea, deciding not to call at the lifeboat pier, but instead to find Fred Harling, and strolled along the sea wall to the second boat crossing.

Fred Harling found them! They heard a voice call as they reached the gap. Harling was standing beside a serried array of lobster pots, holding a number of short lengths of line. As they went up to him, he bent down over a pile of floats and wire and odds and ends, straightened himself again, and said: "This yours?"

In his outstretched hand he held a red dinghy mooring buoy with a white letter S painted neatly on it. Two feet or so of nylon line dangled below.

Peter nodded dumbly. He had searched for the mooring buoy the moment they climbed out of the car, not actually expecting to see it in the broken sea and unsurprised when he failed to do so. The dark color of the water, the broken leaden light, the constant movement were more than enough to hide it. This he was not prepared for.

The other two were quite silent, and he croaked: "Where did you find it?"

"High on them old concrete slabs below Selsey House. Wedged up there, it was. Top o' the tide this mornin', I reckon. Color of it caught me eye." He turned it over and held up the nylon cord. "Reckon it chafed on something."

Peter began to say: "But what?" and checked himself.

Fred Harling stretched out the buoy and, as Peter took it, said: "Better put a wire trace on it next time. You was lucky. Few more yards and it would'a gone right up to Pagham with this wind. Niver've found it then."

"It was very kind of you." Mig found her voice at last. "It was the only one we had."

They stood and talked aimlessly for a minute or two, and

then left Harling and went back along the wall, turning away from the coast up the road.

When they were out of earshot, Peter said: "What d'you make of this?"

The other two were silent.

He held up the nylon line, gathering the strands together between finger and thumb. "It wasn't chafed—it was cut!" The ends of the strands as he held them came together in a straight line.

Chapter FIFTEEN

MIG said, with unusual responsibility: "I still think we ought to tell somebody."

"Such as who?" asked Clinton.

"We daren't go back to Old Mr. Ramidge today. There'd be no end of a fuss."

"Mr. Perrin'd say 'that's funnier still' or something."

"Young Mr. R. . . . ?"

"He's as mixed up as we were over the shifting."

"Mother?" Mig looked hurriedly from one to the other of the boys.

Peter stared back in silence, waited and at last broke the silence. "She's bothered enough about us as it is and she wouldn't understand what it means anyway. *We* don't. Let's go over it again."

Mig groaned.

One by one Peter ticked points off on his fingers. "We aren't in anybody's way. We haven't had a row with anybody. We aren't damaging anything. We aren't even making a noise unless Mig's transistor's carried across the water sometimes."

"I've hardly used it!" Mig was defensive.

"Haven't said you did. We haven't any of us done anything that we know of that could make grownups mad."

"Okay," said Clinton. "So some guy wants us out just the same. Why?"

Peter shrugged helplessly.

"First thing he does, he shifts the mooring. Right? Second thing, he cuts the buoy adrift. Right?" Clinton paused, waiting obviously for a question.

"And?" asked Mig.

"Why didn't he cut it the first time?"

"Hadn't thought of that." Peter bit at a piece of loose string on his thumb. "It would have given us even more trouble."

"It's given us enough anyway. The real trouble is we don't know who he is or why he wants us away. We've gotta work it out."

They were all silent for a long time. Finally Clinton spoke. "Maybe we're wrong. Maybe he doesn't want us away. Maybe he just wants us some place else."

"You mean?"

"Maybe he's got an interest in just that piece of water."

"Why?"

"Search me! But if he shifted the buoy to draw us off from the patch where we were working, he must have had a reason. Think of an important reason."

"He must have known we would go back."

"We didn't," Clinton pointed out dryly. "We didn't because we had a good reason for not going back." He lifted an inquiring eyebrow.

"The *stone?*" Mig's voice went up an octave.

Clinton turned one hand palm up in a gesture of ignorance.

"He *couldn't* have known about the stone?" Mig rushed in again.

"Well, there's not a helluva lot about the surface of this patch of water to make anyone pretty keen about it. So what's under the surface?"

"We've seen nothing," said Peter doubtfully. "Not a damn thing."

"*Yet,*" Clinton answered sharply.

"D'you think they could have found the first cathedral?" Mig looked at him wide-eyed and furious.

"Doubt it." Clinton pulled at his lower lip. "Somebody'd be shouting their heads off if they had."

Peter frowned. "Only if they were archaeologists."

"If they're *any*body"—Clinton cut across Peter's doubts—"anybody legal!"

"Who else would be interested in skin diving . . . ?"

"Smugglers, spies, somebody after Navy secrets. Your Portsmouth's just up the creek."

"Or somebody looking for offshore minerals—oil, magnesium, vanadium; gold, even." Mig had been reading *The Sea Around Us.*

Crushingly, Peter answered: "Magnesium'd be in solution. No gold here. You need a dirty great rig to drill for oil."

"Can't tell." Clinton considered possibilities. "Whoever did it was smart, though. He shifted the buoy. He reckoned we'd go under to look at the mooring. He planted it next to the stone. And then he guessed we'd be so worked up we'd forget about anything else—leastways about anything like a proper search of the whole area."

"You don't think that they planted the stone? That it's a fake?" Mig was outraged.

"Nope. It's been there a good few hundred years." Clinton shook his head emphatically and grinned at her. "Don't lose your sweater! But I *do* think they knew it was there and I think they knew you two were mad about archaeology, and I think they just brought the two things together when they found we were in the way of whatever they're up to—and that's smart." He finished his elaborate sentence with an enormous intake of breath.

Peter nodded, his forehead anxious.

Mig declared hurriedly: "But only an archaeologist—somebody interested in it, anyway—would have recognized the stone. *We're* not sure ourselves even now!"

"Not if they'd seen the same sort of thing before."

"You said you didn't think they'd found the old cathedral!"

"I know. But they may have found *something,* and the point is that they've *not* shouted about it."

"This wind!" Mig was in despair.

Peter disregarded the exclamation. "How would they know we were interested in archaeology?"

"Common sense." Clinton was blunt. "They knew you were at Bosham—gray suit soon found out. They must have known you were working at the cathedral. Everybody knows about what happened at Dover and on the Wall. Probably someone just went and asked what you were doing here. It's easy."

"Let's find out!" Mig was stung into sudden action. "We can get back to the road along the dyke top. There'll be a bus. The Master-Builder hardly ever leaves before six."

"Nobody's asked him." Peter was disappointed. "I thought they'd have gone to him first of all!"

A devious question-and-answer session with Young Mr. Ramidge had ended at cross-purposes.

"D'you think he'll guess that something has happened?" Mig's voice was uneasy.

"We were with him up to half-past two. Doesn't seem likely." Clinton shook his head.

"Don't know. I'm never quite sure what he's thinking. He uses his father as a stalking horse. Doesn't ask direct questions." Peter hadn't made his mind up.

"Got him nowhere fast this time," snapped Clinton. "Where next?"

"Let's brush up against the Dean sort of accidentally and

ask him flat out if anybody's been inquiring about us," suggested Mig.

The Dean was at a meeting. They waited for him and waylaid him in St. Richard's Walk when it ended, between the packed and splendid geraniums. He greeted them with cheerful sympathy and quoted the weather forecast: "Winds southwesterly moderate to strong."

"Mostly strong," said Peter. "We've been down at the Bill."

"By road, I trust."

"By road." Peter made a grimace.

"When are you going to be available to help us again?"

"This is bound to mean an extra day, sir." Peter's voice was genuinely apologetic.

"I see that." The Dean nodded, half turned, and then said vaguely: "I was talking to a friend of yours on Monday—no Tuesday, I think."

"Friend of mine?" Peter looked startled.

"A journalist, I understand. *The Mail,* I think. He was connected at one time with your father's newspaper. Interested in your work."

"Was he on a story, Dean?" Mig butted in.

"General inquiries, I gathered. He said something about a— a 'follow-up' to the finding of the Roman pavement."

"Do you remember his name, sir?"

"Something simple," said the Dean grandly. "Horace— Maurice—something."

"I know a Maurice." Peter's voice was hurried. "Did he have a message for me? Any questions?"

The Dean shook his head magisterially. "Nothing," he declared. "He did ask if you could be considered a qualified archaeologist now."

"What did you say, Dean?" Clinton dashed in to what was clearly a joke.

"I said not qualified, but effective. He was perhaps a little—pressing. He had a—young lady with him." The fine-cut nose wrinkled a little.

"Mini?" Mig's voice was carefully innocent.

"You *are* an extraordinary young woman! Yes, mini."

Peter found his opportunity. "What was *he* like? I'm not sure I remember him."

"Tall, broad-shouldered, dark. I noticed he had a scar over his right eye. Does that help?"

Peter shook his head. "Some of them stay only a short time. I don't always remember . . ."

"The girl was"—the Dean paused and made a vertical gesture with one finger—"very long, very straight up and down. She had this long flat hair. I'm told they iron it."

"They do, Dean," Mig assured him gravely.

"Dear me!" said the Dean.

They stood aside and watched him pass down the narrow walk. When he had disappeared inside the deanery gate, they stared at each other with open mouths.

"Manna," said Mig irreverently, "just manna! We didn't have to ask a question."

"Horace—Maurice—never heard of him! And we got a top-rate description, too."

"And the girl"—Clinton gestured up and down in imitation of the Dean—"without curves."

"That makes three—with gray suit."

"We *know* that they're making inquiries now."

"Suppose the Dean had asked him for his press card?"

"Nobody does. At least we know something that they don't know."

Clinton stopped dead in his tracks. "I was looking for gray suit!" he said, crestfallen. "*They* were there."

"Who was? Where?"

"At Selsey. The third car. There was a man and a girl in it —necking. She had long straight hair."

"Did you see a scar?"

"Saw them from behind—dope! Didn't bother to look twice. I've seen a guy necking in a car."

The Dean reappeared, with one hand raised. "The glass is rising," he called. "Depression moving rapidly to the northeast. Further outlook—fair."

"Thank you, Dean." Mig put real gratitude into her voice.

Chapter SIXTEEN

"EVERYTHING aboard?" Peter's voice was crisp. "Ready with the shackle!" He bent down and pressed the starter button.

There was a sound like a strangled hiccup.

Peter looked startled, hesitated for a moment, pressed the button again—firmly this time—and waited. The self-starter whined, there was another hiccup, the motor stayed dead.

Peter, his voice shocked now, said: "Hang on to the mooring, for the love of Mike! There's something wrong."

"I kinda thought there might be." Clinton allowed himself a touch of sarcasm. "Such as?"

"Starter's busted." They heard the whine again.

"Starter ain't," said Clinton positively.

"What then?"

"Just the motor." Clinton was almost offensively cheerful. "J-u-s-t the motor." He reinserted the pin in the shackle, took two turns on the buoy rope, and came aft. "Open her up, let's have a peek."

Peter began muttering furiously as he opened the casing.

"Naughty!" Clinton made the rebuke as acid as possible. "Let's take a look at the connections."

Methodically he went over the wires one by one, examined the distributor head, opened the carburetor, and said finally: "Nothing on the outside. What about the plugs?"

"It's just been overhauled," said Peter. "Can't be anything

wrong with the plugs! Mr. Callan wouldn't have missed them."
He put his finger down. "New—look! They're brand-new.
And we haven't done more than two or three hours on them."

"Shall I take 'em out?"

"It's just been overhauled," Peter repeated. "My uncle'd say,
'Take it back to them!' We've got plenty of water."

Clinton took his meaning at once. "Tow her up with the
dinghy?"

Mig, with just a touch of self-righteousness, said: "We
haven't touched a thing so it can't be our fault."

"Want to bet?" demanded Clinton.

The dinghy was streamed astern, ready for use. They hauled
it up alongside. Peter took charge of it with Mig. Clinton
stayed in the *Snail*. The outboard started at a touch and
Clinton slipped the mooring. They wriggled a way between
the moored boats, headed into the fairway, and moved up the
harbor to the boat yard.

Mr. Callan himself met them at the slipway. He called over the
water: "Trouble?"

Peter shouted back: "Engine."

"Bring 'er in here!" Mr. Callan indicated a berth. "What
sort of trouble?"

Clinton brought the *Snail* alongside neatly, looked up and
said: "Sort of won't-start trouble."

As Mr. Callan lowered himself into the boat, they told him
what they had tried. Rapidly he went over the same points.
"You had the plugs out?"

Peter shook his head. "No, we thought we'd better bring her
up to you."

"Quite right! Let's take a look." Mr. Callan took out the
first plug, scrutinized it, and held it up for inspection. "Clean
as a whistle." He replaced it and removed the second, and at
once said: "Aaah!" He held up the plug. The points were wide

apart. He said doubtfully: "Could be that and again it couldn't. She been runnin' all right?"

"Perfectly," replied Peter. "No trouble at all."

"I don't see . . ." Mr. Callan wiped his forehead with the back of his hand. "I don't see. . . . Brand-new they were. Took 'em out of the packet an' put 'em straight in." He placed the suspect plug carefully on a thwart and shifted the next one. "Nothing wrong there." He sat contemplating it for a long minute and finally moved to the fourth and last of the plugs. "Ought to've started all the same," he said as he put his weight on it. "Wouldn't go proper but ought to've started." He drew out the fourth plug and held it up. His voice this time was startled. "Now how are you goin' to account for that?" The points in the fourth plug were jammed firmly together. Mr. Callan picked up the other one, held them together and studied them in silence. "Brand-new . . . been runnin' for three four days . . . no trouble . . . and this!" He paused for a moment. " 'Tisn't even as if it was the same with both of them." He was clearly aggrieved. "Packers!" he said at last.

The reference was obscure but Peter took it to mean damage at the factory in the packing. He asked: "Do you think we ought to put in a new set."

"No-o. I'll fix these." Mr. Callan pulled out a small pair of pliers and made the necessary adjustment. Skillfully and with precision, he slipped the plugs back into the cylinder heads, screwed them home, and, replacing the leads, switched on the engine and pressed the starter.

This time there was a coughing grunt. The engine obstinately refused to come to life.

Mr. Callan looked up and stared at Mig.

Peter said: "I think Mr. Callan wants to swear. You'd better go out of earshot."

Mr. Callan laughed. "It's all right. I won't burst. But 'tisn't just the plugs."

Almost two hours later, and with the tide running strongly out, they slipped away from the boat yard, the engine purring sweetly.

Mr. Callan said gloomily as he pushed them off: "Is my face red?"

They were well out of earshot when Peter asked: "All the same, *was* it Mr. Callan?"

"He said he did the engine himself." Mig too was doubtful.

Clinton, lying back relaxed on a thwart, listed the defects: "One plug wide, one plug closed, starter splines greased up, and contact spring on the rotor arm twisted. All in one overhaul? I wouldn't bet."

"One coincidence is enough," said Mig.

Her brother jumped on her. "You can't have one coincidence! I mean, you've got to have two things to coincide."

"We've got three," said Mig placidly, "and that's too much. Who did it?"

"Gray suit. Who else?" Peter's voice was worried.

"Scarface," suggested Clinton.

"Scar's only over his eyebrow," put in Mig. "What about the girl with flat hair?"

"Any or all of them." Clinton nodded. "Someone who's pretty much on the ball anyway. None of them big things. None of them positive. All of them taking time. D'you reckon they wanted us out of the way this morning? Guessed we'd try to handle it ourselves first? Not want to bring the grownups in?"

"Betting that we wouldn't make a fuss. I think you're right." Mig nodded at him. "What about going ashore when we get to Selsey and asking Mr. Perrin if he saw anything suspicious this morning?"

"And start him asking us questions back!"

"Not on your life!" put in Peter hurriedly. "What I don't

understand is why they just mucked about with small things. They could have wrecked the whole engine." He considered for a moment and went on: "They could have sunk the *Snail* at her moorings."

"They don't want a fuss either." Clinton tilted his hat over his eyes. "Let's shut up and think about it."

They reached the inshore end of the entrance channel.

"Keep her right over against Black Point!" Peter's voice was quite unjustifiably irritable.

Mig, who was steering, snapped back: "Plenty of water on the Winner with this tide."

"Keep her over! We can't take any more chances . . ." He hesitated, and then said frankly: "I think I'm scared."

For once neither Mig nor Clinton chose to be flippant. It was Clinton who broke the brief and honest silence. "We got reasons. These guys are nuts."

Peter accepted the "we" gratefully. "D'you think we ought to go back?"

"Oh, no!" gasped Mig.

Clinton shook his head. "Wouldn't do any good. It's broad daylight. They wouldn't try anything now. That"—he nodded at the engine—"was done in the dark. The buoy was shifted in the dark too . . . and the mooring cut. Our best line's to make like we've not noticed any damn thing at all."

"But they know the motor was dead! We must have noticed that at least."

"They'll think that *we* think it's that Callan guy's fault. After all, we've come out again!"

"If we go on down to the new position, they'll think we're just stupid, and that helps." Mig's voice was oddly earnest.

"Perhaps we are," grunted Peter.

"We've got the coastguard on our side and a lifeboat around the corner . . ."

"And it's a perfect day." Mig's eyes swept round the wide channel. There was no frigate today but there were two giant tankers passing each other close to the Nab Tower, and three coasters, and a passenger ship coming down Channel, and seven yachts and a big motor cruiser.

Peter said: "Keep well clear of the East Target!"

Mig nodded, this time without argument.

One of the yachts came about lazily in the light breeze and stood over toward the Isle of Wight. A little flurry of gulls slipped past them, eyeing them without particular interest. The big motor cruiser came up with an important fuss of foam under her bows, drew level perhaps a hundred and fifty yards away, and went off in a flashing of polished metal and another important fuss of foam under her stern.

"Chromium Crate!" said Clinton with lofty contempt.

Peter, with his eye fastened on the hand-bearing compass, said: "Here or hereabouts. Anyway, it's good practice in pilotage. Drop the hook, Clint! Let's check."

They took three-quarters of an hour before Peter was satisfied, and even then he said: "We may be thirty or forty feet out."

"Or yards," agreed Mig wearily.

They were lucky. Peter searched uptide, Clinton astern of the *Snail*. It was Clinton who found the nylon mooring line at the fourth dive from the position that Peter had finally fixed and he followed it up to the heavy grapnel. He surfaced fifty feet from the *Snail* and waved cheerfully. They had agreed to put on maximum signs of enthusiasm for the benefit of anyone with binoculars on shore.

Mig started the engine, Peter tripped the anchor, and they moved up to Clinton. He came aboard by the ladder.

"Cut all right!" He was hanging on to the end of the nylon

line and brought it aboard with him for inspection. There was no vestige of doubt left now. The line had lain quietly on the bottom; it was unfrayed.

"Why?" asked Peter, with his forehead puckered again.

"Who?" Clinton offered alternatively.

"Gray suit?"

"But who's gray suit and why would he do it?"

"It isn't as if anybody else has been diving here except the London Sub Aqua people last year."

"And Mr. Perrin said they were diving mostly outside the Mixon."

"And even if they were here, they wouldn't cut buoy ropes or fiddle about with plugs!"

"Why should they? Mr. Perrin said they were a good crowd."

"Who then?"

"Why?"

"Full circle!" Clinton, shaken out of his customary calm, almost shouted. "The only thing we're agreed on is that they— whoever they are—tried to get us away from the inshore waters. We decided that yesterday?"

Mig nodded.

"Right then! And they aimed at keeping us clear this morning. Agreed?"

This time both Mig and Peter nodded.

"Okay. So we go take a look at the inshore water. Now!"

"We can't." Peter shook his head vigorously.

"Why not? We're here. 'Tisn't their water. No law against it."

"They'll see us from the shore."

"No-o." Clinton pursed his lips and put his head on one side. "I got a plan." He stared speculatively at Mig. "Take your jacket off!"

"I've got nothing on underneath," Mig said bluntly.

"Put something on, then! But I need your jacket."

"What for?"

"Listen!" Clinton had their undivided attention. "I'm going to swim in as near as I can guess to where our first mark was and see what I can see on the way. Peter's going to take the dinghy with a dummy in your jacket and wearing your hood." He stared hard at Mig. "He's going well out so that it'll be quite clear what he's doing on shore. Then he's going to make like he's going overboard and he's going to tuck the dummy in the bottom so they'll be sure there's just one man in the dinghy, and then he's going to carry on boat tending as usual."

The dummy was quite surprisingly lifelike—Mig's jacket had been stuffed with all their sweaters and some old canvas and stiffened by a slat from the floorboards, ruthlessly wrenched out by Clinton. "Your unc won't mind. Good cause." With Mig's cylinder securely strapped in position, it was crowned with Mig's hood. They were sure it would bluff the cars along the front.

They brought the dinghy up on the seaward side and slipped the dummy carefully aboard. Clinton followed it and held the dinghy stationary for Peter. For a moment the two stood upright together, showing themselves convincingly for the benefit of watchers. Then Clinton eased himself gently into the water between the bows of the dinghy and the *Snail*, clung to the gunwale with his fingertips, and watched while Peter, assisted by Mig hanging over the side of the boat, fixed the dummy in position, facing toward the bows.

When it was secure, Peter nodded to Clinton. Mig cast off the dinghy painter. The outboard started, and Peter headed out to sea.

Clinton, still hanging on to the side, watched critically. Over his shoulder he said: "Looks damn good. Bye now!" slipped under, and began to swim strongly inshore.

Mig watched the bubbles as they trailed out on the quiet water. Long before Peter had reached the "diving position" that they had decided upon, they had become invisible.

Clinton had said: "Watch Peter's side! If you spend time staring inshore, it might give them ideas." Mig followed every movement that her brother made. The dummy was extraordinarily effective. They'd even managed arms with an old and brownish sweater. The figure was hunched and purposeful from the *Snail*. From the shore and even through binoculars she was certain that it would fool anybody. Everything depended on how convincing Peter could make the first "dive."

It convinced even her. For a moment Mig thought Peter had actually gone himself—there was a bit of splashing. The next moment the dummy had completely disappeared and Peter was waving gaily to her. She waved back, surreptitiously looked inshore to see if she could see bubbles, couldn't, and turned back to Peter, switching on her transistor radio.

The waiting was interminable. Even the transistor did not help. She heard five numbers in a row and was unenthusiastic about any of them. Finally, there was a Sirens disk that she liked—very noisy, with a lot of drums. She put up the volume.

It was halfway through when she saw the bow wave of the motor cruiser. In the first moment it seemed to be heading straight for her, and she straightened up to yell. Then she realized that it would pass the *Snail* perhaps thirty feet away. She thought: Stinkers! Blinding along like that! Even as the words formed themselves, the bow wave diminished; the noise of the motor cruiser's engines, roaring above the noise of the radio's drums, died away; and the clumsy hull slid past inoffensively, leaving the *Snail* rocking just a little in her wash. From her stern a man waved in friendly fashion, and Mig, with her indignation vanishing, waved back and returned to her task of watching Peter.

The program was improving. She liked the next item too. Peter was doing very well, drifting slowly with the tide, using the glass-bottomed box assiduously. Knowing her brother, she thought that he was probably getting results. After a minute she allowed herself a quick glance inshore. There was a trail of bubbles, but Clinton wasn't due back yet; she decided that they were leftovers from the motor cruiser's props.

She turned her head and watched it for a moment. It was down near the Mixon already and seemed to be turning. She wondered if there was fun in anything as big and as powerful and as clumsy as that, and returned to her watching.

Something bumped against the hull of the *Snail*. Mig lifted her head, heard it tap twice more, and decided it was a piece of driftwood on the tide. There were no signs of Clinton's bubbles yet.

The motor cruiser had turned and was coming back. The sun was hot. The music was sweet now, saccharine. There was no wind. It was almost boring. Even the motor cruiser with its wide, furious bow waves was no longer exciting. Mig knew what it would do—roar up, cut the motors, go past quickly, and start up again.

It did just that.

She hoped Clinton was still well out of the way. Looking anxiously for a moment into the clear green water, she thought she saw the distant uncertain shape of a swimmer, decided that it was imagination, and watched the big boat lazily. Anyway, Clinton would be much too deep for the cruiser to do him any harm.

It passed. She heard the roar as the twin diesels revved up again. A girl leant over the rail aft and waved. She had long, flat hair.

Chapter SEVENTEEN

PETER was a long way downtide now. Mig watched him
patiently. It was costing an enormous effort of will not to look
over her shoulder toward the land to hunt for bubbles that
would show Clinton coming back. She knew that the boys were
right; they had to keep up the pretense of working out to seaward. She was just contemplating the admirable quality of her
patience when there was a thump on the bottom boards somewhere up near the bows and, as she turned her head toward it,
she saw a hand slide over the gunwale, clutch hold and stay
there.

Before she could move level with it she heard Clinton's
voice, triumphant, enormously excited. "We've got it, Mig!
We've got it!"

When she arrived at his hand he was staring up, his face
mask pushed back on to the top of his head, his eyes wide and
excited, all trace of his normal pose of uninterested calm gone.

He said: "Is it okay, Mig?" And as she answered: "Okay," he
said: "It's there all right. I lit on it coming back. Plain as all
get-out—masses of it."

Mig, almost dazed by his vehemence, asked: "Masses of
what? Is it something they've put there? What's plain?"

"Everything!" said Clinton exuberantly. "All that we need."

Mig bent down to him. "Clinton Hammond—cool, man!
Stop shouting and tell! What's plain? What have they got
there?"

He stared at her blankly for a moment. "They? They nothing! I've found your ole cathedral for you. Give Peter a shout. D'you think I could come aboard? I'm pooped."

Mig shouted across to Peter and at the same time shook her head firmly, totally confused now. "What d'you mean the old cathedral? You were looking for . . ."

"Sufferin' cats! Ain't it enough?"

Peter across the water raised his arm in reply. He began to go through the elaborate pantomime of getting somebody aboard the dinghy and raising the dummy again to its sitting position.

Clinton, hanging on to the side of the *Snail,* grumbled: "Tell him to put a jerk in it. I'm cold."

"He can't," said Mig simply. "He's got to do it that way. What d'you mean—the old cathedral?"

"That," answered Clinton bluntly, "just that. Squared stone —piles of it—a bit of a wall—everything."

The dummy was upright now. Peter turned to the motor and started up. The dinghy headed round with a jerk and came toward them.

Mig found herself saying over and over again: "Are you sure? Are you sure?" And heard Clinton answering her mockingly: "Sure I'm sure!"

As the dinghy came up to them, Mig called out: "He's found the old cathedral!" And above the roar of the motor she saw Peter's blank look and made out the puzzled "What?"

In a babbling confusion the boys somehow kept their heads. Clinton came abroad the *Snail* as if from the dinghy. The dummy was broken down into its component parts. Mig's hood and jacket and the sweaters and padding were passed over. And finally, as Clinton collapsed on the warm bottom boards, Peter streamed the dinghy astern and said: "Now— start at the beginning! What's it all about?"

Clinton, with his head cradled on a kapok life jacket, said: "I swam in on the bearing we reckoned for the first mark buoy. Didn't see a thing. Stretch of rock about fifty yards from here, sand again, patches of rock and more sand. Nothing that mattered." He paused for a moment, clearing his memory. "I reckoned I'd about reached it and I turned southwest about fifty yards, I guess, and I saw something pink and I swam toward it and it was just that old gas cylinder. Saw it the first day, remember? It's stuck in pretty deep. Tried to shift it. Couldn't. Fred Harling's put down a pot three four yards away from it."

"Any luck?"

"One lobster in, one lobster near the outside."

"What did you do?"

"Helped him up," replied Clinton cheerfully. "That's the way he wanted to go. Fred Harling helped us."

"And then?" demanded Peter.

Clinton considered the point. "Then I swam down another fifty yards and turned back. Big boat passed around about that time. I reckoned she was too far away to worry about. Sort of slowed down and then went ahead again."

Mig nodded at him. "The Chromium Crate. She was heading down to the Mixon.

Clinton grunted and went on. "I reckoned out where the *Snail* oughta be and I started heading back. Saw it about two minutes later."

"Saw what?"

"Your cathedral," said Clinton mildly. "There it was—all neat and laid out."

"What d'you mean—neat and laid out?"

Lazily Clinton detached the underwater scratch pad from his belt. "Long lines of stones running due east. Lot of squared stones—lot all shapes. Swam along it to the end. Bit of it—

ten, twelve feet perhaps—stacked like a wall." He consulted a rough, almost unintelligible scrawling on the pad and said: "Turned south. Lot of sand then. Covering it. Few bits of stone sticking up—could have been rock, I dunno—but there seemed to be a line on the south again. Bits here, bits there. Then there was a big pile here." He put his finger on the diagram. "Southwest corner, I'd call it. Regular stack. Long squared stones there, and more of them going north again."

"Anything in the middle?"

"Bits and pieces. Wasn't time to work it all out."

"How big is it?" Peter stared at the bare essentials of the diagram.

"Hundred and thirty—hundred and fifty feet. Hadn't anything to measure with, but it's big, boy—it's big!"

"The east end, was it curved?" Mig asked the question almost automatically, remembering what she had read about the early Saxon churches.

"Wouldn't know. There was stone and there was sand. It was a building, that's all I can tell. I'm sure of that—dead sure. Didn't look for anything more. Figured I'd had about enough. I was swimmin' back when I heard that chromium job again."

"It was," agreed Mig.

"And she slowed down same as before. Was that when she was passing you?"

Mig nodded, and began to speak.

Peter interrupted her. "May be chromium but at least they had that much decency."

"They did," said Mig grimly. "The girl on board waved to me. She had flat hair."

Clinton sat bolt upright and stared at her. Peter put his head on one side. They were quite silent for a long time.

Finally, Clinton said: "Every other dame today has flat hair."

Mig regarded him sweetly. "I haven't."

"You're every, she's the other."

Peter said: "Was there a tall dark man with her?"

Mig shook her head. "A short man with red hair and a—oh, an ordinary man. Nothing particular about him. They were in the wheelhouse—couldn't see them properly. How far were you away when she slowed down?"

"Far enough," replied Clinton. "But I screwed down my valve and held my breath—long as I could—so they wouldn't see bubbles."

"I thought I saw you out of the corner of my eye. There was something under water."

"I was way over that way." Clinton jerked a thumb past his shoulder. "Couldn't have been me."

Peter nodded. "He's right, Mig. There could be dozens of flat-haired girls around. They go with chromium. And they slowed down for us each time they passed. The lot that cut our buoy adrift wouldn't do that."

"And I didn't see anything that anybody'd want us to keep away from—not a damn thing," put in Clinton. "Just that old gas cylinder and one lobster pot. Not another flaming thing!" He paused and considered the possibilities. "Didn't cover the whole area," he admitted finally, "but I covered a lot. Nothing there."

Again there was a little silence.

Mig ended it. "D'you think it *could* be somebody who knows about the old cathedral then?"

Peter shook his head. "We've been over all that half a dozen times. If they'd found it, they'd have talked. The papers would have got on to it."

"*If* they were archaeologists," Mig persisted obstinately. "Supposing they aren't archaeologists?"

"What then?" Clinton cocked an eye at her.

"Treasure hunters."

"What treasure?" demanded Peter. " 'Tisn't as if the old cathedral was overwhelmed in a tidal wave. We've been through all that too. It was abandoned because William the Conqueror said it had to be. They'd have shifted any treasures. They did, in fact. They shifted the Lazarus panels."

Mig stared straight ahead, still doubtful.

Peter watched her and added finally: "Maybe we've been wrong all along. Maybe the first mark did shift with the tide. Maybe the mooring line parted for some reason we don't know. Maybe the engine *was* Mr. Callan's fault. If they wanted to get us out of the way, they haven't done much since we came here this afternoon."

"What could they've done?" demanded Mig.

"They could have had an 'accidental' collision or something. They were just polite, that was all. Anyway, we've found the cathedral—that's what matters."

Mig said doubtfully: "I know you're right but . . ."

Clinton climbed to his feet and stretched himself. "I think I'll live," he murmured. "I guess you won't sleep tonight if you don't have a look at it."

Peter grinned back at him. "That's it, and you wouldn't like that. I think if we make a good bit of fuss about putting on our gear and fixing our masks and all that, and then go in over on the seaward side, it'll be all right. If they *are* watching us from the parked cars, they'll just think we're working close in to the *Snail.* Perhaps we've been imagining about the watching too. Our trouble is we're too suspicious."

"Huh!" said Clinton. "Let's go."

They made the last necessary adjustments. Mig stood up once to help her brother and sat down again. Then in turn the boys took up position on the gunwale, slipped over, swam out a yard or two and dived.

Stubbornly Mig kept up the fiction of looking out to seaward. She was still far from satisfied. After a little she searched for the Chromium Crate. They had last seen her passing down the Looe Channel. She found her now to seaward of the Mixon at its eastern end. It was impossible to tell what was happening there, but she could see an occasional splash.

Mig waited patiently. It would have been marvelous to have discovered the cathedral without all these anxieties. Whatever Clinton had found, it would be important. It might not be the cathedral but at least it must be an ancient building, and that would be reward enough for their work. It would have been better if Peter had discovered it, of course; he had been so far ahead of the rest of them in his solutions of the problem—so far ahead even of Old Mr. Ramidge. She wondered what the old man would say when he heard the news. Against probability, she had expected upstanding walls and high windows and doorways—thought of them even while she knew that they could not possibly exist in the circumstances of the destruction of old Selesea. These tumbled masses of stone were the utmost that they could have hoped for. She knew that well enough and yet she was disappointed—and disappointed with herself for being disappointed.

She turned and allowed herself a prolonged inspection of the beaches. There were cars from end to end of the stretch that they called "the front." The low-tide beach was crowded with people. Now that her attention was turned to it she could hear the shouts along the beaches and laughter, and occasionally the punctuation of a motor horn. The crowds were staying late in the heat at the end of the afternoon.

She looked down again at the Chromium Crate. Unquestionably she was fishing. The afternoon was altogether too hot, too peaceful, for suspicion. Perhaps the boys were right.

Chapter EIGHTEEN

PETER looked at his watch. "Half an hour's up."

Mig stared at him critically. "Are you sure?"

"I'm sure," he answered abruptly. "I've only had the one dive today anyway."

Mig turned automatically to Clinton.

The American boy said sarcastically: "He's young, sound in wind and limb, and he don't drink."

"Oh, shut up, Clint!" Mig began to pick up her gear. "I don't want to go if you're the least bit doubtful."

"I'm not." Peter looked back at her. "I'm warm again. I'd say if I wasn't certain."

They put on their gear together. When they were ready, Mig went over first but as they dropped away from the *Snail* she let Peter take the lead, swimming to the right of him and half a length astern. She watched him staring at his wrist compass until he had determined their course.

The whole character of the water was different. They had never dived as late as this before. The sun was low in the west. The water that had been a delicate, limpid aquamarine was blue now. It was still clear. They could still see a long way. She turned her head quickly and stared back at the *Snail*, floating behind and a little above them, but it was as if it was lit now from the sky above them and not from the sun. The bottom had changed color too. The dark patches where the

rocks lay were heavy with deep blue shadows and the green of
the weed patches was deeper, olive dark.

They headed into a sudden shoal of fish which broke, panic-
stricken, in flashes of silver light. A bigger fish hovered almost
invisible out of range, and turned and flashed light as it
turned, and disappeared.

Peter was swimming powerfully but she was aware that she
had no difficulty in keeping up. They had improved enormously in the past few days. She was comfortably sure now that
Clinton was right and Peter would have no problem in making
the swim a second time. She allowed only one tiny nibbling
anxiety to remain—whether he could find the site.

The boys had marked it on their swim with a thin nylon
fishing line and a float that Clinton had cut out of a length of
bamboo they had found in one of the sternsheet lockers.
Deliberately he had made it so small that it would be difficult
to see on the surface—difficult, at least, for anyone who did not
know it was there. They only needed it for the next morning
when they would take, she hoped, a whole boatload of doubters
to the site.

The light seemed to change as they neared the shore and the
depth altered. There was a lot of sand now, and they moved in
a soft white and blue. At times it was awkward to judge direction or, for that matter, speed. Peter was watching his compass
all the time in quick, anxious glances. They carried nothing.
The plan was just to let her see the great stone oblong. There
could be no time for more than that. The boys had measured
it on the second dive—a hundred and forty-five feet by thirty—
but the measurements were rough. They too would have to
wait until tomorrow.

Why had nobody found it before? It was big and clear, both
the boys had agreed on this after the second swim. She had a
sudden inspiration. The height of yesterday's gale had been at

the very bottom of the low water of spring tide. Perhaps the
sand had shifted. The lobstermen had said that the bottom was
always moving, off the Bill, piling up, washing away, scouring
off the rock bed, covering it again. Maybe that was what had
happened with the gale. Her mind flickered over for no particular reason to the gas cylinder. That had been resting on the
surface of the bottom sand when she saw it. Clinton had said
that it was dug in now. Perhaps the sand had shifted there too,
drifting up round it. Odd that a gas cylinder should be so
heavy on the bottom.

There was another shoal of fish ahead of them, swimming on
the same course as themselves. They followed behind it. It was
almost like a pursuit. There was fun in it. Most of the fish kept
steadily in line and steadily at depth. Two on the left-hand
edge of the shoal seemed for reasons of their own to dip up
and down. There was no obvious explanation.

They swam on and on. Peter's head worked on a sort of
three-phase program: a glance at his wrist compass, a long stare
ahead, a side glance back to see if Mig were still there, and
back to the wrist compass. Once Mig managed to make a
thumb-up sign to coincide with the backward glance and Peter
gave her a thumb-up in return. They came to a rock ridge
that lifted perhaps eight or ten feet above the bottom. She
didn't remember it on the chart. It was a slow, easy hump, and
in quick succession she counted eight lobsters in the gullies of
the rock. There was no sign of a pot. Come to think of it, when
Clinton had pointed out the float of the pot next to the gas
cylinder she had seen no other floats between them and the
shore.

It was impossible to tell how long they had been swimming
except by looking at her watch. She had thought that she had
got the timing settled now. When, reluctantly, she looked at it,
she discovered that they had been swimming for eight minutes

only. She knew that it had taken Clinton and Peter eleven to cover the distance.

They kept on. Peter was maintaining an absolutely even speed. Mig felt that she could keep it up for ever. Even though she had been mistaken about the time, she was entirely light-hearted. They had found their "old" cathedral. Clint was wonderful to work with. He fitted into everything. He never criticized, no matter how mad some of their ideas must have seemed to him. The water was warm, surprisingly warm, and the tide didn't seem to be making any difference to them, at least Peter didn't seem to be bothered by it. He appeared quite certain about what he was doing, and even if he made a mistake, she realized suddenly, all they had to do was to pop their heads out of the water and look for the *Snail*. They had almost decided now that there was nobody watching them from the shore. Almost. She felt her own uneasiness creeping back again and dismissed it. Peter made a little sign. She couldn't be certain what it meant, but she thought that it might have something to do with the time and she looked at her watch again and was astonished to find that the eleven minutes were up.

The rhythm of their swimming broke. They saw the stone simultaneously, over to their right at the limit of visibility, and they raised their arms in achievement to each other, simultaneously Peter gestured with his thumb up again, and this time the gesture was triumphant.

They swam toward the pile, keeping level now, and long before they reached it she could see that this was not a natural boulder formation. There were too many straight lines in it, too many squares. Patches of short weed softened some of the outlines. Sand covered the lower tiers. But everywhere there was clear evidence of the chisel; these were man-made blocks.

Mig was suddenly aware that her heart was beating much

faster than normal. Peter swam up a little so that they could see down on to the pile. This, obviously, was Clinton's southwest corner, the corner of the west front of the ancient church. They had argued endlessly as to what had happened. Had the cathedral been built on a bluff? The "cliff" between the West Beach and the Bill was thirty feet high in places but the sea had undermined it, eroding it in the endless succession of the tides, sweeping it away in slice after slice, stopping only when the concrete wall was built, and undermining even that in places in its turn. Perhaps that was what had happened with the cathedral. Perhaps in slice after slice it had been undermined until the southwest front had fallen outward and lain so while the tide sucked out the sand and gravel and the pebbles underneath it, and lowered the heavy stones inch by inch until they reached the bedrock. It must have been an island by itself for a little while, and then even that must have sunk and left everything except the heavy stones washed clear, like a giant sheepfold on the bottom of the sea.

Peter touched her shoulder and swam off up what had been the line of the west front. She swam with him, hesitated, and then broke away, turning up the thousand-year-old line of what had been the nave. As she swam, her memory reached back to Kipling's story of the Conversion of St. Wilfred, and she heard herself singing silently inside her mask with the child in Kipling's story, "O ye whales, and all that move in the waters, Bless ye the Lord; praise Him and magnify Him for ever."

Puck had asked after that if seals were also counted among those who moved in the waters, and St. Wilfred had told them the story of Eddi, his chaplain, and the seal that was called Eddi also. The seal had saved them off this stretch of the coast and afterward Eddi had become the priest of Manhood End, and Manhood was just up the peninsula, and the South Saxons were Wilfred's converts. They had mocked Eddi afterward when he held his service for the ox and the ass, and he had said:

"I dare not shut His chapel on such as care to attend."

And that chapel had been somewhere on the edge of the marshes round the Isle of Selesea, and she was aware that she was almost lightheaded with wonder and excitement, and a consciousness of history all intermingled with the strange, pale blue magic of the light.

Chapter NINETEEN

THE hot coffee was lifesaving. Clinton had made it, knowing that they would be chilled, on the Primus stove that they had never used before. They were all three curiously quiet. Triumph seemed to have drained out of Mig on the long swim back. They hardly discussed the cathedral; it was accepted now. Mig's only contribution was to say: "It had an apse, you know. You can trace the curve of it." And Peter had said: "She's right. The curve's there when you look for it." After that they had only talked about getting warm again.

The beach was almost empty now, the crowds going up the steps with the last of the sunset.

Clinton said: "I adore your mother but I'm glad she's out tonight. We'd catch it otherwise."

Mig said defensively: "She knew we were going to be late because of the tide."

"Not as late as we're going to be. Not half as late. What time d'you reckon she'll be home?"

"The Newcombes are late birds." Mig was beginning to be flippant again. "She'll come home to roost about midnight."

"Time we made a start then," said Clinton.

"Three minutes and another cup." Mig held out the empty beaker.

"All right! Three minutes then. What are you looking for?"

"The Chromium Crate. Ah, still down by the Mixon!"

"Hasn't moved," said Clinton and began stacking away the plates. "Okay, Peter?"

"Okay," Peter answered lazily. "I'm going to sleep on the way up."

Mig finished her second cup. "And did either of you keen-eyed alert young gentlemen see the piece of white stone on the left-hand side of the apse?"

"White stone?" Peter sat up abruptly. "What sort of white stone?"

"Could have been Purbeck limestone."

Peter whistled. "Don't believe it. It's too soft. It would have worn away a long time since."

"All the same," said his sister blandly, "it was white."

"Stop yakking and get things squared away!" Clinton thumped his hand on the thwart. "If we don't get over the bar by dark, we're done."

"Plenty of time," declared Peter confidently. "Can you get in the anchor by yourself?"

"Sure."

They stowed the last of the oddments. Peter went aft, considered for a little, and flooded the carburetor. He called out: "Heave in!" and waited.

After a few moments Clinton called back over his shoulder: "Up and down!" Peter pressed the self-starter with a flicker of apprehension that was a leftover from the early morning. The engine started like a dream.

Over the purring sound of it, he called: "Heave up!" He gave Clinton thirty seconds to get the anchor clear and, reaching down, put the engine into gear. There was a screech of tortured metal. The boat shuddered as if she had been hit below by a violent blow. There was a long moment of furious noise, and the engine went totally dead.

In the shocked silence that followed, Peter heard himself say, quite calmly: "Let go again and give her a good scope."

Mig, in almost the same even tone that he had used, asked: "What do you think it is?"

"God knows!"

Clinton made fast the anchor cable on the samson post and came aft.

Peter said: "Felt as if something hit her an almighty wallop just about below me. I think we've lost the prop."

Mig leaned over, half her body outboard, screwed up her eyes and stared into the darkening water. "Prop's there."

"What then?"

"Tail end shaft's busted?"

Clinton shook his head. "Shouldn't have thought so. The prop wouldn't look right if it was."

"It looks right," Mig insisted.

"One way to find out," said Clinton, and began to zip up the jacket of his suit.

Peter nodded and made his harness ready for him.

"Shan't need flippers. Give me a bit of line, Mig! I don't want to have to be swimming against the tide." He lashed the end of the line round his waist and gave the coil back to her. "I'll shout if I want you to slack away."

He went down the ladder in the stern.

He was back again in less than half a minute, his head and shoulders above the counter, sitting there with one leg through the ladder.

He asked: "You chuck any wire overboard?"

"Not me," said Peter.

"Plastic-covered wire?"

"Not me."

"Dirty great length of it's jammed up between the prop and the stern gland—and I mean jammed up! Seized solid!" He grinned at the two shocked faces staring down at him. "Question: what does B do next?"

"Unsnarls it," said Peter firmly.

"All right! *You* unsnarl it, honey chile! But you're goin' to have to do somethin' about your fingernails after."

Peter looked at him inquiringly.

"It's jammed solid and nothing'll shift it except maybe a hacksaw or a blowtorch. Got either?"

Mig said, with decision: "Two hacksaw blades! I saw them when you were making the float for the new buoy."

"But no saw?"

"No saw."

"All right." Clinton nodded. "Give me one." He examined the blade suspiciously, grunted at last, and said: "Might do. Can try."

Peter asked with a sudden urgency: "But how could it have got there?"

"I wouldn't know." Clinton grinned at him again. "But I'd say that one end was round the prop, the bight had a coupla turns round the shaft, and the other end was fast to the rudder bracket or something."

"You mean, it was done deliberately?"

"I mean, if it wasn't, it was a helluva kind of accident." He glared over at Mig. "Take in the slack soon as I get settled and hang on to it!"

He disappeared. They could hear him thudding about as he settled himself. Afterwards they could feel a thin, delicate, irregular vibration, the transmission of his sawing. He was under for a long time. Finally, they heard splashing and peered over the counter.

He was thrusting one leg through the bottom rung of the ladder. Looking up, he pushed his mask to the top of his head and stretched his other hand up with half the hacksaw blade in it. "Busted," he said. "One more?"

"One," Mig replied.

"Better be careful then."

Mig handed him the second blade. He stuck it through his watch strap, adjusted his mask, stuffed in the mouthpiece of the aqualung, and disappeared again.

"I could've taken over." Peter spoke irritably.

"Better to leave it to him. He's good at that sort of thing. What time does it get dark?"

"Pretty soon."

The sun had disappeared unnoticed, the twilight was crowding them.

This time Clinton was under for a bare five minutes. They heard a surface splash, and three inches of broken hacksaw blade tinkled on the floorboards.

Clinton's head appeared over the stern. "And always on the buttered side!"

"What d'you mean?"

"That it's the long piece that goes down. Can't get at things with what's left—and it's too dark to go down and hunt for it." He heaved himself into the boat and took the towel that Mig held out. "Don't think it'd solve the problems of the world if I *did* free it."

"Why?" Mig demanded.

"The prop looks all right from up top, but it's out of true. The whole bracket's been wrenched over. Time to think of something else."

"Such as . . . ?"

Peter spoke. "I've been working it out. If we towed her in to the beach . . ."

"Tide's risin'. We'd have to hang on to her till midnight nearly."

"If we took her round the Bill and anchored her off the lifeboat station?"

"Would the anchor hold her there?" Mig looked wildly anxious.

"Don't know."

"Either way we look pretty damn silly." Clinton grinned at them.

Peter nodded. "We ought to be able to get out of this by ourselves. We've done it before."

"There'll be an almighty row if we don't," said Mig.

"We're used to it." Clinton's grin was infectious now. "And we've got one more option."

"What's that?"

"Tide's with us. Breeze is comin' up, but it's from the southeast. We could tow her up to Chichester Bar with the dinghy . . ."

"It'd be dark long before we got there," objected Peter promptly.

"There's an early moon. We could anchor and wait for it."

"Take her in as soon as it's light enough." Mig's voice was eager. "Anchor her in sheltered water over the mud."

"Go up to Bosham in the moonlight."

"Beat your mother to it an' collect the *Snail* in the morning."

Peter was already on his feet, rummaging in a locker.

"What're you looking for?"

"Filler. We'll have to top up the outboard's tank and we'll take the spare can."

They were all suddenly alive again. The gloom had vanished. There was no danger. The light southeasterly showed no signs of blowing up. They knew the lights. There was plenty of fuel. The only problem was time.

Mig asked the last question, just to satisfy herself. "What time's moonrise?"

Peter and Clinton answered simultaneously. Peter said: "Half-past nine." Clinton said: "Half ten." Both laughed, and Clinton added: "No cloud."

Mig calculated. "Three-quarters of an hour to get *Snail* in and anchored inside the East Head. Three-quarters of an hour to get up to Bosham, going slow. Twenty minutes to get home. We ought to have half an hour in hand."

"With luck," said Peter devoutly.

There were a number of tasks. The dinghy, to begin with, was not equipped for towing. They had to improvise safe points for securing the towing lines—two of them, because they were not sure of the strength of the available rope. The dinghy tank was two-thirds empty. It was far into the twilight before they were ready.

Peter and Mig took the first turn in the dinghy. The boys had decided that there would have to be two in it to give the light craft weight enough for the task, and one of the boys, inevitably, had to stay with the *Snail* to get up the anchor.

Peter stood up when they were ready and took a swift last look round the lights. The Nab was a splendidly clear fixed point. The Chichester light buoy was not yet visible. It was, he remembered, a good six miles away. They would pick it up in time.

"I'm going to take her out well clear of the Streets and the Hounds, and steer for the Chichester buoy when we sight it. Quick white flash! We can work in to Eastoke Point light afterwards."

Mig nodded. "Sounds right." Odd little prickles of excitement were running up and down her spine. She had put on a thick cardigan under her neoprene jacket, and they had all climbed into their diving pants. It was going to be a long, cold haul.

"Shout when the anchor's off the ground!"

"Will do." Clinton began to heave in.

Peter waited.

It seemed a long time before the sharp "All clear!" jogged

his ear with almost physical force. The outboard started. Cautiously Peter went ahead, taking up the slack of the tow. There was a heavy jerk as they felt the weight of the *Snail*. Then suddenly they were running smoothly, the outboard had settled to a steady level roar, and the lights on the shore were beginning to slide silently past them.

On the *Snail* Clinton stowed the anchor carefully, ready for an emergency. When he was satisfied, he lashed the battery lamp to the little flagstaff in the bows. It wasn't regulation but it would have to do. The light of it reached the dinghy even in the last of the twilight. That was comforting anyway.

Chapter TWENTY

THEY lost the West Bay lights surprisingly rapidly. Peter was heading out sharply into the deep water beyond the Streets. It was full dark and more than a quarter of an hour later before they sighted the quick nervous flash of the Chichester buoy. It was irregular for a few moments, dipping below the horizon. After that, it was a steady flicker.

He had been heading a little too far out. Slowly, Peter brought the dinghy round until its snub nose headed midway between the flash and the half-visible lights of the Hayling Island shore. He gave the tiller over to Mig. "Keep her there," he said brusquely.

Mig took the tiller and answered: "She tows pretty well."

"Sweet as a nut." Peter's voice was exultant. One by one his doubts had vanished as they got clear of the shoal water off Selsey, as they got the feel of the tow, as they picked up the light of the Chichester buoy.

The only nagging doubt that remained was whether they should have gone inshore with the dinghy before they left and telephoned . . . . Who? Not Mr. Perrin. He'd have said, "Beach her!" Not Mr. Eartham. He'd have said, "Anchor her off the lifeboat slip." Not Mother. Mother would have flapped and said, "Come home *now*. Get a taxi!" Old Mr. Ramidge?

Certainly Old Mr. Ramidge. They could have telephoned him. They could have told him about their troubles. They could have told him about the old cathedral. They could have told him anything, and he would have said, "Decide for your-selves."

Peter turned it round in his mind for a little while, snapped suddenly: "You're heading in too much to the land!" and realized that they were doing just what Old Mr. Ramidge would have told them to do.

He looked at his watch—still three-quarters of an hour to moonrise, and they'd need a good twenty minutes after that to get any real light from the moon. He turned round and watched the bows of the *Snail*. She lurched rhythmically a few degrees from side to side. Otherwise she towed well. He could see no signs of Clinton.

He heard him four minutes later. "Something coming up astern!"

Peter whipped round again. Whatever it was, the *Snail* masked it. He put his hand over Mig's on the tiller and pulled it slightly toward him. The dinghy headed over to starboard, pulled clear of the bulk of the *Snail,* and they both saw simul-taneously the red and green side lights and a moderately high white light above them. Peter straightened the dinghy up on course.

"Biggish boat," he said. "Must've come through the Looe channel. At this time of night?"

Mig said, with absolute conviction, all her fears suddenly crowding in on her again: "It's the Chromium Crate."

Peter considered this with great care and answered reluc-tantly: "Could be."

"Now I *am* scared!"

Peter peered at her in the darkness, troubled. "I still don't think . . ."

"I do!" Mig's voice was almost angry. "The buoys might

have been a happening. The engine couldn't have been. Tom Callan wouldn't . . ." Her voice trailed away.

The silence grew between them until, almost as if he were being forced, Peter muttered: "And now this."

"It couldn't have been an accident either. I've been thinking. Something knocked against the boat a little after the Crate passed that first time, and I know I saw something underwater. I didn't do anything about it. I was watching the Crate coming up from the Mixon. I thought it must be Clint, and then there was the Crate and the girl, and I saw her hair . . . I didn't look again."

There was another long silence. Peter said, very carefully, at length: "They could have dropped somebody as they came level on the way down—somebody to fix the wire so that it would twist into the gap between the prop and the stern gland, and he could have just hung there till he heard her coming back and swum out and got aboard when she slowed down, or hung on anyway until they were clear."

"Wasn't politeness." Mig's voice was flat. "What do we do now?"

"We could cut loose, pick up Clint, and try to get into Chichester entrance first."

"Would we?"

"I don't know." Peter was painfully honest. "The Crate's pretty powerful. This isn't." He slapped his hand on the rounded cylinder on the port side. "I'm very nearly sure she'd overtake us before we could reach the entrance."

"Could we go over The Winner at this state of the tide?"

"We might be able to."

"Could she?"

"I don't know. I just don't know, Mig. I think the only thing we can do is to carry on and wait till they start something." He slowed down the motor until he could shout clearly across to

Clinton. "I think that's probably the Chromium Crate."

Clinton's voice came back: "I'm sure it is. Wasn't anything else down that way."

"Got any ideas?"

"Nary a one."

"We carry on then. Wait and see." Peter's mind flicked round and round like a squirrel in a cage. Beyond all doubt the Crate was bigger, better equipped, faster than they. Faster even than the outboard would be without the *Snail* in tow. She was the sort of ugly brute that looked as if she could do between thirty and forty knots before she shook herself apart. If they cut loose from the *Snail,* what would she do? Run us down as like as not!

He thought that he had said the words to himself, but Mig said, surprisingly: "I think they would too."

Out loud Peter asserted: "At least we're nippier than they are. We can turn on a sixpence. They'd have a devil of a job. I think we could always get inshore of them if we were put to it, and run her up on the beach." He was encouraged by the idea, oddly relieved. They would lose the *Snail* and probably smash up the dinghy, but they could run inshore anywhere along this coast and disappear. There was always that for comfort at the back of things.

He could see the masthead light over the bulk of the *Snail* now. The Crate—if it was the Crate—was coming up fast. He stood up precariously, one hand on Mig's shoulder. He could see the bows of the *Snail* and Clinton's hunched back and shoulders as he watched the oncoming boat, and behind him he could see the Crate—there was not the slightest doubt about it now. She was lit up like an ice-cream parlor. Above the noise of their own motor he could hear the deep, rumbling sound of the Crate's diesels, and above that again, pop music on a very loud speaker.

He throttled down the outboard for a moment and called urgently to Clinton: "If we have to cut and run for it, stand by to jump! I may not have time to warn you."

He squatted down again on the bottom boards of the dinghy. The Crate was towering above the *Snail* now. He saw Clinton come up to the bows and turn the big torch so that it shone astern.

There was no reaction from the big motor cruiser. She came thundering on. Peter could see the spray of her bow wave lit in the beam of the *Snail*'s lamp, spreading up into two gigantic curves of spray. Her wheelhouse windows were dark. The light was behind on her afterdeck, the music was there too. It was impossible that there could be another "accident," that the man at the wheel might be dreaming, might at any rate not be keeping a proper look-out. It was surely impossible that she could be coming blindly on automatic control. Big boats, he knew, carried this sometimes. Supposing she was coming up completely unconscious of them. Clinton had only just turned on the light. Where were the flares? His mind went back to the moment when Old Mr. Ramidge had asked them about flares far back in the house on the hillside. Would Old Mr. Ramidge be looking out now? He realized suddenly that the flares were on board the *Snail*. He wanted to kick himself. This was stupidity—the one thing that they had not thought of—the one thing that it was truly dangerous not to think of. He let the thought go abruptly. He could test the accident possibility at least.

He said to Mig: "Bring her round to port. Easy now—easy!"

The dinghy sheered away and the bows of the *Snail* turned obediently and began to follow her. From the motor cruiser, less than twenty yards astern of the *Snail,* a loud hailer boomed: "Are—you—in—trouble?"

Was it another accident then? The change was too abrupt. Peter could not take it in properly. A moment ago the Crate had been a threat. Now she was offering assistance. He felt a cold sweat all over himself, the palms of his hands were chilled; he had not realized how worked up he had been. The bows of the Crate were well outside the curve of their course now. He heard the roar of her engines diminish suddenly to a deep pulsing note.

The voice on the loud hailer was infinitely clearer now, loud enough to be heard over their own motor, undistorted by the diesel noise. Somebody seemed to have switched off the pop music. The voice asked: "Engine trouble?"

A searchlight from her wheelhouse roof flashed on and the beam settled over the outboard. They were blinded by it but there was nothing hostile about it. It was meant to be helpful.

The Crate was level with the dinghy now and perhaps forty feet away. The voice asked: "Where are you heading for? We'll give you a tow in."

Peter called back: "We're all right. We'll make it. Just some bother with the boat's prop. We'll go into the harbor with the moon."

"Wind's coming up," said another voice. Through the glare of the searchlight they could see that somebody had come out at the side of the wheelhouse. "Glass is going down with a thud. We'll take you in." It spoke as if the matter were settled. "You can't risk going aground with a rising southeaster. The Winner can be a nasty place."

Peter called back: "I know, but we're sure we can do it. We're all right."

"Nonsense!" said the man's voice. "You've got a girl on board. You can't risk it with her."

Mig turned into the light. "I'm used to it," she said derisively.

A girl's voice aboard the Crate said: "You come aboard and have a hot drink. You must need it."

Afterwards neither of them were certain how it had been done, but there was a sudden roar on the big boat's motors. It ceased as suddenly, and she was directly ahead of the dinghy, flirted expertly into position. Peter switched off the outboard with one quick flick of his wrist. As she lost way, the *Snail* came up behind her. Automatically Peter turned to fend her off. In the same moment two men bent down over the stern of the Crate and took Mig's arms. A second later she was on the solid deck. It had happened so quickly that she had had no time to protest.

The smaller of the two men said: "Now, that's better. Pass us your towlines! No, give me the painter of the dinghy first!"

In the turmoil between the counter of the big cruiser and the bows of the *Snail,* half-blinded by the disappearance of the beam of the searchlight, Peter found the painter and held it up. There seemed to be no alternative.

Above him, the voice said: "Pass me the towlines now!"

Peter felt for the end of the starboard line—it was made fast round the thwart—cast it off, and handed it up.

The voice said: "Is that what you were towing on? It'd snap at the first strain. Take this!" A heavy rope was placed in Peter's hand. The voice said again—it was authoritative, commanding: "Take it aboard your boat and help your mate to make it fast. Smack it about now! We can't waste time out here."

Again there was no alternative. Peter put his leg over the *Snail's* gunwale.

"What's it all about?" demanded Clinton.

"Don't know, but they've got Mig aboard. It was like a disappearing trick. Make this fast! We've got to hang on whatever happens."

In the darkness they fumbled, cleared the lifeline from the samson post, made the new rope fast, passed one end round the thwart to make certain, and shouted back to the Crate: "All fast!"

There was an answer that they could not distinguish, and the big boat went ahead slowly, paying out the towline until they were perhaps thirty feet astern. Then they felt the *Snail* gather way. She fell into line in the wake of the cruiser and moved faster and faster until her bows lifted.

Clinton said: "But how did they get her?"

"I still don't know. I was fending you off. She didn't object or anything. They were"—he paused, considering the matter —"they were being nice to her. I think they were being nice to her. I don't know. They're heading up the way we were going anyway." His eyes had moved round until they found the flash of the Nab. "Maybe they're not crooks. Maybe they really thought we needed help."

"Maybe we did," grunted Clinton.

Peter was silent for a long time. "If they didn't," he said at length, very slowly and very angrily, "she's a—hostage."

Chapter TWENTY-ONE

MIG, on her knees on the narrow afterdeck of the Crate, craned her head up and saw the girl with the straight hair towering above her. She said, without even a sign of hesitation: "Oh, thank goodness! I'm so cold—I didn't think—will the boys be all right?"

The girl ignored the question. "You kids shouldn't have been out here as late as this. It's dark."

It was exactly the thing that anybody might have said—anybody grown up. Mig found herself lost again in the mixup of probable and improbable. She dared not hesitate; she chose instantly and blurted out: "We've had a horrible day! Everything's gone wrong. But everything! We should have been in hours ago and . . ."

The girl interrupted her. "What was the trouble?"

"A piece of wire." Mig decided that the truth was the proper card to play. If she tried to invent reasons, they would know instantly that she was bluffing. "It wound itself round the propeller or something, Clint said. Oh, it was awful! I was scared that it would smash a hole in the bottom." She decided it might pay to invent just a small addition. "We can't think where it came from—unless it got caught up in the rudder or something at the boat yard."

"Which boat yard?"

"Bosham." No point in denying that either. "That was this

morning. That was the start of the day. The engine wouldn't go."

"Why?"

"Everything! There was something wrong with the plugs, and then it was the"—she mouthed the word doubtfully—"the splines or something . . ." She left it at that. She was a girl, she couldn't be expected to know details about engine trouble.

A man's voice behind her asked: "What were you doing off the Bill? We saw you there earlier."

"Skin diving." Mig's voice was delightfully candid. "My brother thought that we ought to look for the Cathedral under the Sea. We've just finished training for skin diving."

"And did you find it?"

A small adjustment of the facts wouldn't do any harm, Mig decided, but there was no need to waste truth. "We found a tombstone—at least we think it was a tombstone. You see, we laid a mark buoy where we planned to search and it floated away with the high tide or something." She heaved herself to her feet, turned and took a quick look at the *Snail* moving on top of her own double plume of spray a little distance astern, and asked: "Do you *really* think they're all right?"

The girl said: "Come on below and have something hot. They'll be fine."

One of the men took her arm and helped her forward. There was no compulsion. There was, in fact, no sign of hostility of any sort. Mig was still suspended between the improbable and the probable.

The aftercabin was surprisingly big. The seats and the curtains were in psychedelic colors, the cupboard tops and the cocktail cabinet were in bright formica, the bulkheads had way-out pictures, painted directly on their surfaces. There was a great deal of chromium even here.

The girl mixed cocoa and hot water from an electric kettle

clumsily—Mig decided that she was not galley-trained for yacht cooking—and passed the mug over. She said awkwardly: "You don't seem to have done so well."

"We're awful." Mig confessed it happily over the hot cocoa. "We're trying to learn . . ." She paused, hoping she had given the right impression of irresponsible incompetence.

The man behind Mig said: "Ought to have had somebody out with you!"

Mig turned toward him and declared with a moan: "That would have spoiled everything!"

"Tides are dangerous along this coast. Did you tell the coastguard what you were up to?"

Instantly Mig knew that the question was loaded. Truth, she decided, always stick to the truth—when possible. "We told Mr. Perrin; I think he's the chief coastguard or whatever . . . and we told Mr. Eartham, he's the lifeboat man—the coxswain, I think."

The man, the short redheaded one, asked, perhaps a shade too quickly but still Mig wasn't sure: "Did you tell them that you'd broken down?"

"No." Mig put her front teeth over her lower lip in acknowledgment of innocent error. "I know we should have. But we didn't. We thought we could tow the *Snail* home with the dinghy." She decided to allow herself a little defiance—the child against the grownup. "We could've too! Are you going to take us right up to Bosham?"

"Not Bosham," replied the man abstractedly. "We're staying at Portsmouth. We berth in Langstone harbor. We'll take you in there. Question of tide . . ." He threw the explanation in unwillingly.

Mig was almost certain now. She felt that a protest would be appropriate. "Mother will be so worried," she offered.

"You can 'phone her from the house." The girl was coldly

soothing. "We'll be there before you would have got to Bosham
—the rate you were going. We'll take you back in the car."

Mig decided to play the idiot child for the last time. "It's
awfully kind of you," she murmured. "We're giving you *so*
much trouble."

The girl looked at her, vaguely suspicious, and seemed to
change her mind.

The red-haired man asked: "All right to let her look round the
boat?"

The girl nodded. "Perhaps she's just a little fool. She doesn't
know anything. I told Slim they were ordinary kids, playing
adventures."

The red-haired man shook his head. "They don't seem so
ordinary to me." He scratched his neck. " 'Tisn't our say-so
anyway—the boss lays it on the line!"

"Hold them for forty-eight hours"—the girl was evidently
quoting—"or till the third run's over."

"You been to South Binness Island ever?"

"Why?"

"Helluva place! Nobody ever goes there. Nothing but scrub
and sand and one old houseboat—wrecked. You won't like it."

"Nobody else ever goes there?" she asked.

"That's why!"

"If we knew one way or the other . . ." Peter was beginning to
let his anxiety show.

"We don't. So we act like it was the worst case. That's
ordin'ry sense."

"How *do* we act? They've got Mig. If we try anything . . ."
He left the possibilities unspoken, and added after a silence:
"And we can't just leave it to her!"

"We can," said Clinton, "and we've got to. She's got us out
of worse jams. She'll get word to us—sooner or later."

"How?" asked Peter with more than a hint of despair in his voice.

"Nothing we can do yet." Clinton's tone was sharp. "Wait till she gets the word across or till that thing slows down."

Peter allowed himself to break away from his watch on the afterdeck of the Crate and turned to the stuttering flash of the Chichester light buoy. He was uneasy. Over his shoulder he said: "Something queer somewhere. Wish I knew what our course was. I've been watching for Mig."

He had a moment of inspiration, hunted for the Pole Star, found it, looked back at the winking light, and muttered hurriedly: "Due south of us, just about. We ought to've turned up for Chichester entrance five or six minutes ago. We must be heading for Portsmouth! We've got to stop him . . ."

Clinton put out his hand. "Squat!" he snapped. "He said he'd tow us in. He didn't say where. We didn't either. We agreed that we'd wait for Mig to give us the high sign. At least he isn't headin' out over the Channel! Let's see where he tows us."

The wheelhouse was full of oddly shaped cubes and bars of light, some of them pale green, some a faint brownish red, flickering; the motor cruiser was elaborately equipped with gadgets.

The man that Mig hadn't been able to describe was steering. He asked: "You all right?"

"There's nothing wrong with me." Mig's voice was light-hearted. "Is that the Chichester buoy?"

"It is. You know this water then?"

"Not very well." Mig was aware of Redhead behind her. "We live in the North, but we've got an aunt who lives in Midhurst and an uncle who lives at Bosham." She had decided to overwhelm everybody with unnecessary information. "Are the engines very powerful?"

"Very," the helmsman answered in the indulgent manner of someone speaking to the altogether ignorant.

"Could I see them?"

The helmsman said: "Take her down, Charlie!"

Redhead agreed uncertainly: "All right. I dunno though . . ."

"Just a quick look." Mig guessed a little wheedling would do what was needed. "I don't know anything about engines really." She was determined to see over the whole boat.

Redhead led her to a companionway aft of the wheelhouse. It was brilliantly lit below. She could see two enormous high-speed diesels, between them a third engine, smaller—possibly a cruising engine. The big pair were working—thunderously.

Between them was a man bent almost double, reading a gauge. He wheeled round as Redhead called.

He had a white scar—very prominent in the bright light—over his right eye.

As quickly as she dared, Mig asked if she could go "up into the bows." Redhead agreed, and they went up, to stand in the rush of air over the roaring double arc of the spray.

Mig called to Redhead above the noise, conscious that her voice had a tremor in it and glad that the darkness hid her. "It's marvelous! How fast can she go?"

Redhead said cheerfully: "Thirty-five knots—if she's pushed."

"Wonderful!" Mig's answer was full of all kinds of meanings. How was she to get away? Redhead was unsuspicious now; perhaps she could push him over the side as they went aft. She considered the idea seriously, facing into the wind, her eyes filling with water that was close to tears, and abandoned it. He would shout as he went over, and they would hear him—there were three men as well as the flat-haired girl, and for some reason that she could not explain to herself, it was the girl Mig was afraid of.

Redhead said: "Okay, let's go aft!"

Mig mouthed "Yes" and followed meekly. She had no doubts left now—and no ideas either.

They stopped outside the wide doors and the short flight of steps that led down to the aftercabin. Mig decided that she would have to talk, and talk fast. She began to expand herself on the wheelhouse and the big diesels, and she went on from them, unhesitating, to the beauties of the spray and the rush of the wind over the bows.

The girl, looking up at her, winced a little at the enthusiasm. Twice she tried to interrupt her—Mig in full spate was unstoppable. Finally, the girl said: "Shut up! I've got a message for you, Charlie." She turned to Redhead.

Mig said apologetically: "I'm awfully sorry. I talk too much." She looked from one to the other brightly—too brightly—and murmured in what was perilously close to being a parody of a young girl being tactful: "I'll go and see how the boys are getting on."

Neither Redhead nor the girl answered her.

She went aft down the narrow side deck, her heart beating faster and faster.

Suddenly she knew exactly what she had to do. There was enough light from the afterscuttles of the main cabin to see what she needed. The tow rope to the *Snail* was made fast over the mooring bitts on the starboard side. It had four turns on it and the conventional half-hitch. She supposed that it would be tight, difficult to cast off. It wasn't. It came off in twelve seconds —perhaps less. She left one turn on and hoped for the best. The dinghy line was secured to the bitts on the port side. Oddly, it was more difficult than the big rope had been but it came clear after a moment of desperate anxiety. Standing up, she hung on to it with half a turn round the starboard bitts, freed the heavy tow rope and let that go; then, passing the end of the dinghy line under the afterrail, she scrambled over it and, hanging on desperately to a stanchion, lowered herself toward the dinghy.

It was towing at a wicked angle. She felt the curve of it under her feet, felt it give, got her feet to it again, and let go the stanchion and the rope at the same time. She was aware that she was terrified. The Crate seemed to heave itself forward in a wild, roaring lunge; then she was half in the water, half in the dinghy, half-lost in the turmoil of the wake of the motor cruiser, half-seized with panic.

Peter said in the strange, almost unbelievable silence: "She's in the dinghy. She must be!" He stood up. "I'm going in."

"Wait!" said Clinton. "She's tough. Minute or two in the water won't do her any harm if she didn't make it. We're still moving."

The *Snail,* vastly heavier than the dinghy, was still running up in the wake of the Chromium Crate. Clinton, automatically hauling in the heavy tow rope, watched her with cat-like care. "She hasn't turned. Can't have spotted anythin'—yet." The big boat was almost half a mile away now.

"There she is!" Peter's voice was overwhelmed with relief. Mig's white face was quite clear in the darkness above the indistinct blob of the dinghy. "Give me the heaving line!"

"Wait a minute! She's still too far." Clinton dropped the wet rope, fumbled for the heaving line, and, going aft to the tiller, put it gently over to starboard.

The *Snail's* head swung slowly. The dinghy was dead ahead now. Peter stood up, steadied himself against the thwart, and swung the small weight at the end of the heaving line experimentally. He could just reach the dinghy, he reckoned.

He swung it twice more and let go. It was impossible to see it in the darkness. But out of the darkness he heard Mig's voice, indignant: "You hit me!"

He laughed aloud with relief and began to haul in.

Chapter TWENTY-TWO

AS the dinghy neared them, Peter called urgently: "What d'you want us to . . . ?"

Mig's voice cut across his: "Get the life jackets! We'll have to make a bolt for it."

"How?"

"With the dinghy, stupid!" Mig could visualize everything. She'd been long enough on the Crate to know what they were up against. "Scarface is on board. They weren't taking us to Bosham . . ."

The dinghy bumped alongside. Peter made up his mind instantly; he knew that he had to trust Mig. "Let go both anchors, Clint! They'll hold the *Snail* as soon as she drifts in to the shallow water. She'll be all right, with luck." He grabbed for his duffle bag, found it, and called: "Here!"

"Flashlight?" demanded Mig.

"In the bag. No time to get the big one unlashed."

"Hurry—she's turning!" Mig's voice was almost desperate. Clinton snapped: "Both anchors over!"

"Get in!"

Clinton snatched at a small bag with personal belongings and half threw himself into the dinghy.

Mig called urgently: "The flares!"

Peter, about to follow Clinton, hesitated. "What flares?" he asked confusedly.

"Starboard locker. Hurry! Oh hurry!"

Providentially he found them at the first groping, thrust them into Mig's outstretched hands, shot over the *Snail's* gunwale into the dinghy, answered Clinton's "Okay?" with a breathless grunt, and heard the dinghy outboard roar into life.

"Which way?"

"Straight in!" Peter stretched out his arm, automatically finding the long dark gap of the Chichester entrance.

Clinton settled on his course, and, turning, searched for and found the lights of the Chromium Crate. She was, he judged, still the best part of half a mile away, but she was heading straight for them. He could see the red and green of her sidelights and the white of her masthead light dead between them. He shouted: "Shall I slow right down?"

"Why?"

"Less chance of seeing our spray. Mebbe we could slide clear . . ."

"They've got radar," said Mig. "I saw it—all sorts of gadgets —probably night glasses too."

"Keep her going!" Peter's shout was positive.

Clinton shouted back: "She's turning inshore of us!"

The alignment of the lights was for a moment completely revealing; the big cruiser was heading on a course between them and the land.

"Trying to cut us off!" Mig's voice was clear above the roar of the outboard.

"Can she?" Again Peter was prepared to trust Mig's judgment.

"She can do thirty-five," Mig shouted back.

"How d'you know?"

"Asked 'em."

There was a gap in the exchange, not a silence—silence was impossible in company with an outboard motor. Peter was flogging his brain wildly.

Mig broke it. "Could we go over The Winner?" She was

prepared to trust that treacherous sandbank sooner than the people of the Crate.

"Wouldn't make it," Peter flung back.

The Crate was much closer already; her sidelights brighter, the masthead light higher from the water.

Clinton bellowed: "Let her come up an' jink round suddenly. We can spin in our own length. Drive her nuts!"

Peter grabbed at the idea. "Gain a bit inshore each time." There was a ray of hope in it. He shouted: "Okay!"

As he shouted, Mig said sharply: "Her *lights!*"

There were no lights. Where the triangle of red, green and white had been there was only darkness and the faint loom of the double white plume of her bow wave on the dark water.

For the first time Peter felt a shiver of fear go down his back.

"Doused 'em." If it was possible for a shout to sound thoughtful, Clinton's did. "Means business," he added.

It was quite clear now that they could not hope to get to the entrance channel first, or reach even the doubtful protection of the Winner. They could not hear the Crate's engines above the high, harsh burr of their own, but it was certain that her bow wave was higher, angrier than it had been in the daylight. She was hurtling toward them.

Peter put his mouth close to Clinton's ear. He had made up his mind. "Turn away—bit to starboard." He waited till he judged that they were almost exactly on the big cruiser's course and then snapped: "Steady! Hold her like that till she's close. Head in for the shore then. When she turns to cut us off again, spin round and cut in under her stern and aim for the Winner. She'll need a lot more room to turn in than we do and we'll make a bit of distance—inshore!"

"I hope!" Clinton nodded his head.

The motor was running perfectly. Peter remembered that they had topped up the tank just before the Chromium Crate had caught up with them for the first time; the spare can was

more than two-thirds full. At least they had no fuel worries—
speed was their problem! He watched the growth of the big
boat with awe. They could see her over the great twin curves
of spray now. The flaring bow, the pile of the wheelhouse,
even the mast was clear against the lazy luminescence of the
Hayling lights and the glow of Portsmouth beyond.

When ought they to begin their attempt? Too soon would
be as bad as too late. How quickly could Clint turn at this
speed? It was easy to turn an inflatable over going flat out—
and they *were* going flat out. Peter pulled at Mig's life jacket;
they had all donned them now. The neoprene of the diving
suits would keep them up in the water, but the life jackets
meant real safety and he was sure they were going to need it.

"Lie down!" he ordered. "Hang on to the floorboards!"

Turning, he watched the Crate again. She was almost close
enough now, he judged—coming up very fast indeed. He
prodded Clinton. "Inshore—now!"

The dinghy heeled wildly as Clinton put the helm down.
Peter had grabbed a lifeline, steadying himself. He watched
intently, saw the instantaneous response of the Crate, and as
the big boat heeled to her own turn, saw the starboard plume
of spray flung up against the stars. Unhesitatingly he bellowed
"Jink!" in Clinton's ear.

The American boy said tersely: "Yup!" and spun the
dinghy. For a heart-stopping moment she was almost vertical,
planing along on one side of the wide, inflated tube. He judged
it beautifully; a little more, Peter knew, and the dinghy could
have gone over. Clinton had far more experience than he had.
The American boy held her now to the curve, the prop practically out of the water, judged the second moment flawlessly,
and brought her down again on to a course that would take her
past the stern of the Crate. As he did so, he shouted: "Hang
on! Wash!"

They smacked into their own wake, porpoised violently,

crashed down with a teeth-rattling jar, and bounced furiously through.

"Hang on!" Clinton's warning was anxious. "Hers'll be a heck of a lot worse!"

The big boat was coming round already. There was no doubt that she was well handled; but there was no doubt also that she had lost ground. They slammed into her wake ferociously. This time the dinghy lifted clear like a leaping salmon, and the engine jarred and shuddered. She hit the water again, drunkenly, buried the starboard side of the blunt bow, took on water, covered them with spray, and then shook herself like a dog.

In shattering bumps she lurched across the big boat's stern and thrashed out over the wash to the calm water beyond.

"Done it!" called Mig exultantly.

All three watched the hull of the big boat, sweeping around in a wide curve on their starboard quarter. It was clear enough that they had gained ground, but Peter, calculating as best he could, was suddenly aware that it was not enough. It was a long way to the Winner and farther still to Wittering beach.

This time the Crate swept in determinedly inshore of them. First the Portsmouth lights silhouetted her, then she began to wipe out the Hayling lights stretch by stretch as she gained on them.

Clinton shouted, his voice uneasy: "She's very fast, and she turns well. Can't try that again—yet! We lost ground in her wake!"

"What then?"

"She's riding us off."

"What d'you mean?"

"Goin' to lie between us and the land and use her speed to ram us if we try anything." He put his finger on the controls.

"What're you doing?"

"Speed doesn't matter any more. We can't outrun her—gotta outthink her."

The noise level diminished astonishingly as the overdriven outboard ceased to strain. It became almost possible to think connected thoughts. They watched the big boat wordlessly as she moved farther inshore and finally appeared to settle on a course.

"D'you think she *would* ram us?" Mig questioned.

"Mebbe she just wanted to ask if we were happy?" Clinton's voice was dry.

Mig, her hair wet and bedraggled from the hectic moments in the Crate's wake, shivered, but not from cold.

They ran like this for nearly six minutes, watching the big cruiser intently, turning over in their minds the possible ways of escape.

Peter said at last, without confidence: "If we ducked in astern of her again, say, about level with the coastguard station . . . ?"

"She'd turn in with us and smack us as we passed. She's tough." Clinton was altogether positive.

"If we turned in before that—level with the Hounds and she hit the rocks?" Mig asked belligerently.

"Tide's well up," answered Peter. "She'd probably get across. Anyway they've got charts—they're not fools. Probably that's why they're heading us out."

Clinton nodded. "Keep on keeping on," he offered bluntly. "And watch out for happenings. If we slow down a bit now, he'll maybe think there's somethin' up with the motor. Few knots in hand could come in useful to us sometime."

The long empty stretches of Bracklesham Bay began to change to the lights and glow of the West Bay trailer camps. It was hard to be patient. Safety was ashore, barely a mile away—friendly coastguards, lifeboatmen, police, ordinary human beings. Mig was aware for the third time that she was frightened.

It was Peter, however, who broke the long pause. "Let's chance it! Cut in suddenly. Mig was right about the Hounds; perhaps they'd be useful just because they're there. He might be scared to run in too far to head us off."

"Helluva gamble," said Clinton warningly, "but I'll try anything once. When?"

"Now!" said Peter firmly.

Clinton put the helm over, simultaneously putting up the throttle to its maximum. They were gathering speed before the turn was complete, racing toward the long, level beach. It was Clinton who recognized the speed of the Crate's turn. She too, apparently, had something in hand.

The crisis was on them before they knew it had begun. The Crate had turned inshore on her heel, now she came back at them with monstrous power. Clinton, intent on the shore line, reacted too slowly. Peter's shout was insufficiently clear. Suddenly the great curve of the Crate's bows was above them, the roar of her bow wave overwhelming them.

Almost too late, but still in complete control of himself, Clinton put all his weight on the tiller. Largely, the dinghy saved herself. The sharp bows missed her. Even as the bow wave roared in to overwhelm her, she suddenly slid sideways, the curl of the wave pushing her away. They grazed the side of the Crate amidships, were flung violently to starboard, Peter's duffle disappeared, half the loose gear was gone, but as the blunt, unlovely stern passed them, they were still afloat—and the outboard motor was still roaring!

Astern of them the Chromium Crate came around in the darkness, still inshore of them, still in command.

"We've got to get help somehow—and quickly!" Peter's tone was near desperation.

Caustically Clinton shouted back: "Okay by me!"

Mig, only just picking herself up from the water slopping over the floorboards, gasped: "Old Mr. Ramidge."

"You all right?" Peter asked urgently.

"Old Mr. Ramidge!" insisted Mig, and pulled out one of the yacht flares that she had jammed in under her half-inflated life jacket.

"I'd forgotten . . . " Peter almost snatched at the ten-inch cylinder. The instructions on its casing were invisible but he thanked his stars that he had spent twenty minutes memorizing them, going through a sort of dummy drill over and over again with his eyes shut. "Tear off red tape." He almost shouted the words. "Tear off green tape." The green sealing flung away in the wind of their passage. "Pull away striker release . . ."

The blinding red light suddenly obliterated the night. The Chromium Crate was on the starboard quarter, barely forty feet away; they were heading northwest again toward the Portsmouth lights. The flare blazed and blazed: the Crate came in closer and closer. The night was full of noise and movement, of spray and confusion.

And then abruptly it was dark again, and in the instant Clinton put the helm down and spun the dinghy once again.

Peter fell, half on top of Mig, grabbed at the floorboards and clung while the dinghy raced round and headed once more for the Bill.

Chapter TWENTY-THREE

THE house was furious with the ringing of bells. Old Mr. Ramidge had tripped the switch of the fire alarm, he was clanging a small stand-by hand bell, and the pendant bell push over his favorite sitting place in the center of the great window was pushed hard home.

As his son hurled the door open, the old man—his voice incredibly strong—snapped: "Ring the lifeboat station—Eartham! Those three are in trouble!"

"What three?" Young Mr. Ramidge was unprepared.

"The Manson youngsters! Use your intelligence! Tell Eartham they're burning a red flare—they may be on the Hounds. They were towing their big boat earlier . . . Get on with it, man! Get on with it!!"

The red brilliance flickered, gave a last pulse brighter than anything before it, and was gone. The night was, for a long moment, almost intolerably black.

The flat-haired girl shouted with a hot and malignant anger: "You mucked it, Mike! Now everything on earth'll be snarling round here in ten minutes."

The man with the scar bellowed back at her: "Shut up! Damn thing spins on its heels like a top. How was I to know they had a flare?"

"You tell that to the Big Man . . ."

"*You* let the girl go!"

The redhead outroared both of them. "Lay off it! They're trying to head in again. Keep 'em clear of the coastguard station."

"Get 'em away from the land altogether. The lifeboat'll be charging out round the corner any minute now!" The girl's voice was harsh and brutal.

Scarface pushed up the throttles, and with an enormous roar the twin engines went into full speed.

Mig, her eyes full of spray, wiped them desperately and stuttered: "Oughtn't something to happen?"

Ironically Clinton shouted back: "Too quiet for you here?"

"Idiot! On shore—the lifeboat. I mean—oughtn't there to be a signal or something?"

"If they saw the flare . . ."

"Watch it!" Peter's voice warned him. "She's increased speed —again. I think they're going to try to force us out."

Like a punctuation mark there was a bright flash in the sky somewhere over Fisherman's Beach.

"Maroon!" Peter's relief was clear. "Lifeboat's warned."

"I still can't see anything." Mig's anxiety overrode it.

"Give 'em time! 'Tisn't a fire engine."

"They'll come." Clinton's tone was uncharacteristically comforting. "What's she doin' now?"

"Closing." Peter was crisp. "Head out to sea a bit—we'll have to in the end anyway. Let's give him what he wants now and see what happens. We mustn't try jinking in again until we absolutely have to. We must wait till we see the lifeboat."

Young Mr. Ramidge came back into the big room and automatically switched on the light.

"Put that damn thing out!" His father's voice had the venom of a snake's hiss. "I'm trying . . ."

Young Mr. Ramidge could see his father hunched above the

big telescope. He apologized and went on without a pause: "Coastguard had already reported it. They told the lifeboat it was a motor cruiser on the Hounds!"

"Did they?" Old Mr. Ramidge snorted.

"They're testing a new inshore lifeboat at Selsey. They've sent it out. Be much quicker in this weather. Eartham's waiting to see if they need the big boat."

Old Mr. Ramidge's wheelchair shot backward from the big telescope like an angry cat. "Take a look! See if you can see white in it—white streaks moving fast. Right to left!"

It took Young Mr. Ramidge a long minute to adjust his eye. "Come on—come on! You'll lose it! Get out of the way!"

"Aah!" His son disregarded him. "Something there—something moving! What . . . ?"

"That," said Old Mr. Ramidge with acid emphasis, "is the motor cruiser the coastguard thinks is on the Hounds."

"What d'you mean?"

"There's something very wrong . . ." The old man's knees pushed his son away from the telescope.

"I'd love another cup of coffee," said Mrs. Manson. "No brandy. I've got to drive. Do you think I ought to phone my youngsters?"

Across the coffee table her hostess said: "Mine hate being checked on."

"The young do." Mrs. Manson laughed. "Mine are at least civil about it, though. They ask tenderly after my nerves—or my hangover, or whatever. Perhaps it's more insulting."

Everybody laughed.

The son of the house laughed with them and asked: "Shall I 'phone Mig? She's quite old enough to appreciate it, and I can ask how they got on today."

"Inspiration!" murmured Mrs. Manson, picking up her cup.

"And I don't even need to get out of my chair. Ask her if they've found anything worthwhile."

"What are they looking for?"

Mrs. Manson shook her head. "It's terribly important but I'm not sure that I understand. They explain from time to time, but it's all above my head."

The conversation shifted amiably. Mrs. Manson was describing the subtle avoiding action that the children used whenever a visit to their aunt was mooted. Most of those present knew their aunt: all of them sympathized.

In the middle of the laughter the son of the house came back. "No joy!" He caught the last joke and laughed too. "No answer. I'd say they weren't home yet."

"They didn't fix a time." Mrs. Manson was entirely tolerant. "I thought they didn't want to so I didn't press it. It takes quite a while to put the boats to bed, I understand. At least it's been used as an excuse on three evenings already. They'll be in."

"I get ants," said her hostess.

"Mine are older. I get ants sometimes. But they've promised to keep out of trouble."

"Ought to've seen the lifeboat's lights by now," said Mig uneasily. "She'd be showing lights, wouldn't she?"

Peter called back: "Yes! Give her time! Got to get the crew together. I think I've got an idea."

"Shoot!" said Clinton.

"Suppose we edge down a bit, toward the Mixon. Last time the Crate swung round *inshore*. That's how she nearly got us. Right?"

"Okay."

"If we edge in to the Mixon and jink at the right moment, she won't be able to turn to port. We can get clear under her stern."

"And smash up on the rocks?"

"Not with the tide as high as it is. But she won't be able to ram us—or to follow us. They'll never risk the Mixon, in the dark—even at high water. She'll have to go round to the east end. We'll have a sporting chance!"

"Not bad," said Clinton approvingly. "Not bad."

"Try to spot the Mixon beacon!" said Peter hopefully. "We might see it against the glow of the moon."

"Ride the little swine off!" The girl's voice was as harsh as broken steel. "The last run's due in an hour. We can't have lifeboats fooling around!"

"Edge 'em off too much, they'll run alongside something in the deep-water channel—one of those damn Navy boats doing night exercises or something. Then we'd really be in the dirt!"

"They seem to be coming in a bit. What do they think they're doing? Trying to force *us* on the Mixon?" Scarface laughed brutally.

"Don't fool with them," snarled the girl. "They've foxed you once!"

"As long as *we* know where the beacon is." Scarface leered at her.

"Had it on the radar for the last five minutes." Redhead put in his word. "Ought to pick it up with the glasses any time now."

"Still don't see why they're edging in." The girl was unappeased.

"Gettin' tired." Scarface's voice was wholly malignant. "When they're tired enough . . ."

"Get Jim Shawcross!" The old man's voice was becoming stronger. "All right! Chief Superintendent Shawcross. Tell him someone's been interfering with the Manson children— he'll know about them—at sea—off the end of the Selsey road.

Tell him they were towing their boat up to Chichester entrance at dusk and that they were back this side of the Hounds well after dark. Tell him it was they who burnt that flare and that they did it by arrangement—with me!"

Young Mr. Ramidge said: "What have you been up to?"

"None of your business. Get on with it! Tell Shawcross he *must* get a helicopter from Thorney Island to search for two craft moving fast without lights just south of the Mixon."

"Done it!" shouted Clinton exultantly. "She's going on. Can't turn for a hundred yards—more!"

"Watch the beacon!" Peter's warning was urgent. "Keep well over to port. I don't know how much water there is."

They raced over the fringe of the reef. The gaunt iron beacon seemed to move with tremendous speed past them. In a moment it raked across the face of the low-rising moon. Then they were over. The surge and fall away of the water over the rocks was astern of them and they were in clear water again.

"Head for the lifeboat station! There'll be a crowd there."

"If we can make it," answered Clinton grimly. "What's she doing?"

"Turning to port." Mig's voice was high and precise. "She's going to follow us in."

"Sweat it out," said Clinton.

The distance seemed interminable. Astern of them, picking up the light of the moon now, the big white cruiser came roaring up. There was nothing they could do save wait. In a little while she was level with them, forty yards to port. It was obvious that she was going to herd them out again.

Peter put his mouth to Clinton's ear. "Edge away! Forget the lifeboat!" He waited for a little while and then snapped: " 'Nough!"

The big boat was a fraction slow in responding. They gained

ground. Three times the manoeuvre was repeated. They were well north of the lifeboat pier now, running parallel with the shore and just clear of the moored boats off the beach. The cruiser was a little abaft the beam, waiting, it was terrifyingly certain, for their inevitable attempt to turn in to the beach. Waiting for the moment to pounce.

Peter grabbed Mig's shoulder. "Can you see the shingle crane? Give me a flare! Tell me as soon as you spot it!"

"I see it!"

"Turn in, Clint! Be ready to turn out again when I shout."

He pulled the striker release, and the world was red again.

Chapter TWENTY-FOUR

THE Crate came racing in, poised for the kill. "Get them!" the girl was screaming. "Get them now! Get them!"

For a moment they were aware of the bulk of the cruiser, bigger than ever in the close glare of the flare. They could see her every detail—the mast, the wheelhouse, the big inflatable dinghy swung up on the single davit. Then suddenly the bow wave flung up. The bow itself rose like a porpoise breaching. There was a rending crash, and the motor cruiser heeled over on her starboard side. The big diesels stopped in a scream of tortured metal that reached them even over the noise of their own motor.

Peter shouted: "Out! Head out!" and was aware that Clinton had already put the helm over.

They scraped across the shallows of the second of the shingle banks and slithered, breathlessly relieved, into deep water again.

Thoughtfully Clinton eased the outboard. He said, his tone full of wonder: "You *planned* that!"

"Didn't have time to tell you. Passing the moored boats I suddenly remembered the way the shingle banks stretched out to sea level with the grab crane. I hoped *they* wouldn't."

Mig asked: "Will they be all right?"

"I hope not." Clinton's voice was shaken clear out of its usual humorous calm. "I sure hope not!"

"Look!" Mig's voice went up an octave.

A huge tongue of flame leapt over the shingle bank. Black smoke surged from it, towering with incredible speed against the stars.

Clinton said coolly: "That'll teach 'em to chase small dinghies all around the creek!"

Peter felt himself shaking all over. He asked aloud: "But *why* did they do it?"

"Do what? Run aground? Because they were nuts."

Peter shook his head. "Why did they try to kill us?" Suddenly he wanted to be sick.

"Because we stumbled on something so goddamn big they couldn't let us go."

"But *what*? We've got to get back to the lifeboat station and tell the police." Peter found it difficult to get a grip on himself.

"Hold it!" Clinton throttled back until the outboard was barely purring. He said sharply: "Thought so. Listen! They're not dead—anyway! Reckon that's that big outboard they had in the slings. Guess we'd better be on our way—fast!"

Scarface snarled: "What did you bring that gun for?"

"It's still the best way." The flat-haired girl flung the answer back. "If you'd let me use it off the Mixon, we'd be clear now. One load of buckshot in that dinghy and she'd have run clean under."

"Running down a dinghy, even with a bunch of kids in it, *could* be manslaughter. Using a gun's murder!"

"So what? We'd have got life at the worst—out after ten years. What d'you think the Big Man's going to do with us? He told us he'd 'put down' anybody who fouled this deal. There's a quarter of a million's worth of the stuff at the Harting cottage still and another thirty thousand in the last three shipments. What d'you think he'll do when he hears it's gone?" She jerked her forefinger across her throat. "Those he fixes don't come out after ten years—or ever!"

Scarface ignored her. To the redhead he shouted: "Straight on—Charlie!"

"*I* watched them at least," said the redheaded man sardonically. "They went on along the coast. They don't waste time. You were an outsize nit to fall for that!"

"That blasted flare blinded me!"

Clinton demanded: "Could we land here?"

"No houses." Peter's nerve had come back with the sound of the pursuit. "Passed the last of them. We can't go back now. There's a shingle ridge above the beach; swamp inshore of it —deep swamp, reeds and mud. There's one track across it, but I don't know if we could find it in moonlight."

"Where then?"

"Pagham Harbor." Mig's tone was utterly confident. "There's enough moon to see the entrance. We could lose ourselves anywhere inside, the tide's in."

"Certain?"

Peter said: "Don't know that we've got any choice. They're coming up fast."

"St. Wilfred was wrecked off Pagham," Mig flung back over her shoulder. "Maybe he'll bring us luck—*he* got away with it."

"We'll need it!" Peter was grim. "Why are they *still* chasing us? They must be *certain* we know something."

"What?"

Still crouched against the end of the telescope, Old Mr. Ramidge demanded: "What does he say?"

"Shawcross says they're in very real danger!" His son moved

uneasily closer to the old man. "He says he has to know what you know about it. Now!"

"Nothing," said Old Mr. Ramidge; "except that somebody's been shifting their mark buoys. What does Shawcross know?"

"That the police, Sussex and Hampshire both, know that there's an enormous smuggling coup working up and they think that these children have stumbled on it."

"They're not children," said Old Mr. Ramidge. "They're intelligent and they're tough—and that's not a small boat burning down there!"

"The helicopter reported a big cabin cruiser aground and on fire on the shingle banks."

"A-a-ah!" Old Mr. Ramidge took his eye away from the telescope. "And what would they have been smuggling?"

"Drugs," replied his son savagely. "Cannabis resin, amphetamines, heroin, Shawcross says—fantastic quantities. The information's from the French side. They don't know where it's coming in—or how!"

Mig, concentrating desperately on the uncertain surfaces of the moonlit shallows, called: "In a bit more! That sandbank where we saw the sandwich terns is just about level with us. The deep water goes in past it . . ."

"They're halfway through the entrance channel." The warning in Peter's voice was urgent.

"Can I turn *yet*?" Clinton overbore both of them.

"Bit more—bit more! Now!"

Clinton brought the dinghy on to a course for the break in the dark massed trees of the Church Norton skyline. "Can they see us?"

"I can see *them*," said Peter simply.

"Then we just gotta get ashore first."

If we can reach Norton Priory . . . get there to phone the police . . . Mig thought ahead.

"They've turned!" Peter's words were a shout.

"Be aground in a minute . . ." Mig watched the angled black shape above the spray with a wild anxiety.

Clinton's eyes were fixed on a notch in the trees along the shore. For a full minute the two boats raced in together. It was already plain that Mig had been wrong; the pursuers had water enough to run straight in. It was becoming painfully plain that they would be cut off from the Priory and the road.

Peter saw the danger first. "Down a bit." He gestured firmly to Clinton. "Not too much! We can still get to the church-yard."

Suddenly the trees were rushing up to them. Clinton's fingers hovered on the controls. There was a glimpse of a crescent of shingle. The motor cut, and in a rush of water and spray and the grating fury of the shingle, the dinghy slithered up the beach. The three were thrown forward, floundered for a moment, then Peter said: "Leave everything. Run!"

They were aware of figures pounding down the narrow strip of beach.

They ran!

The metallic voice of the helicopter pilot was distressingly clear on the loudspeaker at the lifeboat station.

"Nothing moving off the coast as far up as Bognor. Thought I glimpsed something in Pagham Harbor but I must have been wrong—nothing moving there now. I'll try out to seaward of the fire again. Over!"

They heard control answer him.

One of the men asked: "D'you suppose John Eartham heard that?"

"He'd be listening," said a voice gloomily.

The narrow meadow was like pallid gold in the moonlight. The three were skirting its eastern edge, searching for the path.

They moved close together in a compact bunch, ready to break through the tangled scrub at a signal of danger.

Mig whispered: "They're watching us."

"Shut up!" Peter's whisper was scarcely audible.

The contrast between their silence and the earlier roar of the dinghy's motor was in no way comforting. They had land under them, not water, that was all. Everywhere the night was full of eyes—and they could not see their enemy. Everywhere there was possible danger.

Peter thought he saw movement and whispered: "Freeze!"

They waited. After a long stillness he saw movement again. Suddenly it was clear against moonlit water, a gap in the seaward tree fringe—in the middle of the gap, the girl. As they watched, something glistened in the moonlight. Then, unbelievably, they saw the gun as she raised it slowly to her shoulder.

Peter gasped: "Down!"

But even as they fell he saw a scuffle. An arm was flung against the girl, the gun spun out of her hands and crashed into the undergrowth. The girl snarled and let fly a string of curses.

Peter gathered himself together. "Run for it up on to the Mound—*now*!"

Behind them the man was saying: "Bitch! Use that and we'll have all the neighborhood on to us. Keep straight now or I'll smash you!"

Mig found the gap that led to the old Roman earthwork next to the rotten tree bole on the edge of the meadow. They crashed up it in the darkness, missed the long mud holes of the ditch and stopped, breathing hard, on the summit. Below them they heard feet pounding hard on the unmade road from the water. The sound stopped suddenly. A night bird exploded in a flurry of angry squawks.

In the silence that followed they heard Redhead's voice: "You can hunt kids all the blasted night. I'm headin' for South Harting. Somebody's got to shift the stuff!"

In the distance, like a line drawn under his words, they heard the high-pitched wail of a police siren.

Harshly over it Scarface snarled: "The fuzz! Already!"

Redhead jerked out: "On the main road. We still got time. Snatch a car from one of the houses. They don't lock 'em in these parts."

"Get these kids first! Stop them talking." The girl's voice was utterly evil.

Peter pulled at Mig's arm. "Was there a third flare?"

Dumbly she fumbled inside the life jacket that she hadn't discarded.

Peter took the flare and said thankfully: "Bless you! Get across the churchyard wall. You too!" He touched Clinton. "Hide between the gravestones they stacked here when they made the new churchyard. You know where they are. I'll join you." His head was flung back, searching the tree above him. "Jump to it!" He began to think.

High in the topmost branch he lashed the last flare, using the lace of one of his sneakers. For a moment he listened carefully but there was no sign of the enemy. Then, very cautiously, he pulled the striker release.

For the third time the night about them blazed with scarlet light.

The voice from the helicopter said with a rising excitement: "Flare burning—Church Norton—St. Wilfred's church bearing two-seven-five degrees—distant two hundred yards—over!"

On a different wavelength the patrol car radios passed on the message. "Patrol cars A30 A31 B42 proceed to Church

Norton investigate red flare. Possible three suspects. May be armed. Do *not* use sirens."

Between the gravestones Mig heard the wail of the nearest siren trail off and cease. There was no sign of Peter. The flare was dying. The night was beginning to fill with noises. She was entirely afraid now. She put out her hand and touched Clinton, and the American boy, sensing her fear, whispered quickly: "Okay, I'm here."

"D'you think Peter . . . ?"

"He's all right. We'd have heard otherwise—long since. Listen!"

There were feet running in the lane; then the sound of more feet somewhere, Mig guessed near the churchyard gate. They heard voices calling and a confusion of curses, and then Peter's voice, high and clear: "Don't let her get away! Stop her!!" Then the whole of Church Norton erupted in a pandemonium of police cars and whistles and shouted orders.

Clinton rose between the headstones and said placidly: "I guess we can now give ourselves up with dignity!"

The sergeant announced without a flicker of humor: "Two more skin divers, sir."

In the glare of the headlights, still in their diving kit, with lifebelts over all, they looked wildly improbable. "Like something from outer space, I suppose," said Mig afterwards.

Chief Superintendent Shawcross stared at them grimly. "You've given us a vast amount of trouble," he began and then abandoning pretense of severity, "and I don't know what we'd have done without you!" He addressed himself directly to Mig. "*You* had the flares?"

Mig relaxed like the winner of a race. "Is Peter all right? Have you got all three of them?" she demanded, running the questions together.

"Two," replied the Chief Superintendent. "The girl and a tall man with a scar, and your brother's in good shape. He told us there was a third, a man with red hair. We're looking for him."

Mig said: "You may find him on the road to South Harting."

"Why South Harting?" There was a new urgent note in the policeman's voice.

"I heard him say so. He said, 'Somebody's got to shift the stuff!' "

"South Harting!" The Chief Superintendent jerked round. "That's the break we needed. Sergeant, get Midhurst and Petersfield—ask them to set up road blocks—all four roads into South Harting. McCrae, get Thorney Island! I want the helicopter to search the fields between here and the bridge. Get a car to the bridge—stop and search!" He turned suddenly and murmured, almost embarrassed: "Bless you!"

Mig asked urgently: "Oh, please—what's it all about? Why were they trying to murder us? Who are they?"

"Drugs," said Chief Superintendent Shawcross soberly. "Half a million pounds' worth of LSD, cannabis resin, and heroin—all the filth. It left France ten days ago. *We've* been trying to find it ever since. We know it's been coming ashore. We don't know where. What *was* it you saw?"

"Nothing," said Mig flatly.

"You *must* have!" The Chief Superintendent's tone changed again; it was abruptly hard and insistent. "You realize you mustn't attempt to hide anything?"

"Of course." Mig was too tired to fight back. "We're not kids. But we saw nothing. All we know is they tried to—to chivvy us away from where we were working. Shifted our buoys, cut the marker adrift. It made us mad!"

"That's what you told Old Mr. Ramidge?"

"Yes."

"Settles that," said Chief Superintendent Shawcross. "They

must have *thought* you'd seen something then. Any ideas as
to what it could have been? Another boat? Something floating?"

Clinton took up the answers. "Not that we saw. There were
big ships farther out . . ."

"Something—under the water then?"

"Nope. Nothing that was suspicious. An old iron bedstead,
cans, a coupla bottles, junk. Oh yes! A busted gas tank.

"We found the old cathedral," said Mig. "At least we
think . . ."

The Chief Superintendent brushed it aside. "Nothing that
could have been used to smuggle stuff ashore?" He paused for
a moment, and getting no answer, turned to Mig. "Did you see
anything out of the ordinary in the motor cruiser? Your
brother told me . . ."

"More gadgets than I've ever seen on one boat."

"What sort of gadgets?"

"Radar, television, depth recorders, logs, all sorts of things.
Radio—VHF, ship-to-shore stuff."

"Stuff you hadn't seen before?"

"No, but *more* than I'd ever seen before." Mig's forehead
was wrinkled. There was one thing—she wondered if it was
important—but the Chief Superintendent had demanded
everything. She asked: "What's a Low Frequency Sound
Transceiver?"

"A *what?*" Shawcross almost barked.

Clinton put his oar in. "They use 'em to talk to fish. There's
an experimental place in the Bahamas—Tongue of the Ocean
or some place. My pop told me about it."

"I still . . ."

Clinton began to talk rapidly. "They don't have to be big.
Could you put one, say, in a gas tank? The cylinder I saw was
heavy. I couldn't shift it. Suppose they used it as a beacon?

Brought the stuff in to there, got it ashore afterwards."

"How?"

There was a brief silence. Clinton broke it doubtfully. "There was a lobster pot right next to it . . ."

"No! Open wickerwork. Besides, there are always too many people on Fisherman's Beach."

"Sir." The sergeant had come back. He cleared his throat. "There was a case, five years back. Dorset somewhere. Watches, it was then. Came ashore in lobster pots. They bored long holes in the bottom timbers."

"I've forgotten—if I ever knew." The Chief Superintendent was incisive. "Who fishes in that area?"

"Fred Harling," said Mig promptly.

"Known?"

The sergeant shook his head. "Been here about eight months. Bought out old Alf Lowndes. Quiet. Doesn't mix a lot."

"He cut our buoy adrift!" Mig joined in again. "Said it had chafed loose. It hadn't—it'd been *cut*."

"Bring him in!" snapped the Chief Superintendent. "Put a couple of men on his shed. Keep everybody away from his pots!"

Mig felt suddenly totally limp. She asked: "Could we phone my mother?"

"I'm sorry!" The big policeman's manner altered completely again. "I've been treating you like a man." He took her arm with a surprising gentleness. "I think we'll call that a proper compliment. Your brother's phoning her from the Priory. We tried to tell her earlier, but she was out."

"I'm glad," said Mig with difficulty. "She'd have been a bit worried."

"A bit!" The policeman suppressed a laugh. "Here he is."

"You all right?" Peter allowed his voice to be gruffly affectionate. "I'm glad. I took a chance and told Mother you were."

"Huh!" grunted Clinton.

"She's coming to fetch us."

"Holy Pete—you've done it again!"

"Done what?" asked the Chief Superintendent.

"They talked her into driving them backwards and forwards to Selsey."

"Selsey . . ." The big man made a quick gesture. "What was it you said—something about a cathedral?"

"Selsey Cathedral—we've found it," said Mig slowly, "but everybody was so busy . . . It's about three-quarters of a mile south of the end of the road . . ."

"And a little east!" said Peter.

ABOUT THE AUTHOR

David Divine was born in Cape Town, South Africa, and has traveled to almost every corner of the world. He has been a journalist and a war correspondent, and was awarded the Distinguished Service Medal for services with the small boats in the Dunkirk evacuation of 1940.

He is the author of numerous books of fiction and nonfiction for adults and children. Among them is *The Stolen Seasons,* another adventure story about Peter, Mig, and Clint.

Mr. Divine now lives with his family in London, England.